The Overtaking

By: Victorine E. Lieske

For my husband, Charles, who supports me through everything.

Chapter 1

Shayne slammed the car door and sprinted up the walkway, a gym bag slung over his shoulder. The late afternoon breeze tossed leaves across the pavement as he stepped up to his mother's house. The larger sun had already set; the second cast long shadows across the lawn. He slipped his key into the door and turned the knob.

Mom, he telepathically called out, *I'm home*.

Her usual greeting didn't come as he entered the house. The smell of something burning made him cough and he covered his nose with his arm.

"Mom!" he yelled. "What'cha doing? Are you trying to burn the house down? You don't have another crush on a fireman, do you?"

Still no answer.

Shrugging, he threw his bag on the worn couch and stalked into the kitchen. The smell almost gagged him. He opened the oven. Smoke poured out. He grabbed a hot pad and pulled out a black smoldering mound. Shaking his head, he tossed the pan on the stovetop and turned off the oven. If her head wasn't attached she would leave it somewhere and then wonder why she couldn't scratch her nose. He smiled. That was his mom.

He clicked on the holographic television, flopped down on the couch and stretched his long legs out in front of him on the coffee table. A bright yellow piece of paper caught his attention and he picked it up. In his mother's flowery writing, it said, "Have you asked a girl to the dance yet?"

With a roll of his eyes he tossed it back on the table. Nice one. His mother should know by now that dancing wasn't his thing. Besides, who would he ask? She meant well, but every time she tried to get involved in his love life, or lack thereof, it kind of made his skin crawl.

A soda commercial played and he put his hands behind his head, trying to relax and not think of anything in particular. The television screen went blank and a split second later a reporter standing in the street came on. The wind blew her short hair as she spoke.

"Terror is ripping through the community here in Hailsburg this afternoon with city-wide reports of sudden disappearances."

Cold fear gripped Shayne's stomach.

"Hundreds of people have been taken," the reporter continued, turning to look at a vehicle behind her. "This driver was even taken while stopped at a cross walk."

Mom!

The Overtaking

He reached out in his mind, feeling for her thought signature. She wasn't anywhere nearby. His hands shook and he felt sick. No, please, not his mother. With his father gone, she was all he had left.

Closing his eyes, he flexed his mental abilities. He allowed his thoughts to glide over the city. Sifting through the orchestra of voices, he tried to find hers, like picking out a single instrument. She wasn't there. He reached farther, now noticing the distressed thoughts of others across the country. It wasn't just in Hailsburg; people were missing across the continent. He focused, rubbing his temples, but it was no use. His mother wasn't anywhere.

She'd vanished.

***

Shayne stepped up the stairs to the large stone building, past the armed guards, and placed his hand on the smooth metal plate fastened to the wall. The plate warmed under his touch and the stone wall shimmered and dematerialized before him. His eyes adjusted from the bright sunlight as he entered the Central Offices. His footsteps echoed through the spacious hall as he walked toward the main marble staircase. Several Council Members stood in their crisp, dark purple uniforms, chatting in hushed tones.

Shayne nodded as he passed, and then hurried on his way to the second floor meeting room. It had been two months since the first attack, or so they called the day the Dykens came and began kidnapping Maslonian citizens. His jaw tightened as he thought about his mother. They hadn't found her, nor anyone else. She was the main reason he agreed to quit school and join the Council.

The door to the meeting room stood slightly ajar. His stomach dropped as he passed the *Council Members Only* sign attached beneath the textured glass inlay. He attempted to swallow the lump forming in his throat.

Upon entering the empty room the thoughts and feelings of the other Maslonians in the building vanished from his mind, leaving an uncomfortable silence in their wake. The room was incased with trimeninite. He pulled out a chair and stared at the seat. It was just like a newbie to arrive first. Should he sit near the front, or would that make him look too eager?

Just as he was about to shove the chair back and walk around to the end of the long table, Senior Council Member Hereth bustled through the door, followed by several others. Conrad Hereth had served as the Senior Council Member ever since Shayne could remember. He hadn't changed much in the last eighteen years either, except for his receding hairline scampering to the back of his head, leaving a clean, shiny surface in its wake. The hair he did have on the sides of his head he kept short, much like the rest of him. Shayne felt tall and lanky standing next to Hereth. He slid down into the chair.

"Mr. Bartlet," Hereth said to Shayne as he set his briefcase down at the head of the table. "I'm glad you're here. You'll make a fine addition to the Council."

"Thank you, sir."

As the rest of the Council filed in, Shayne shifted in his seat. At only eighteen, he was the youngest appointed member. He became consciously aware of his spiky blonde hair and streaks of highlights while observing everyone else, and wondered if he should get a more conservative cut. He rolled his eyes. He'd have to dye it gray to fit in with this crowd.

Several members patted him on the back as they passed.

Hereth cleared his throat when the last member entered and closed the door. "First, I would like to welcome our newest addition, Council Member Bartlet, to the Council." Murmurs of approval echoed through the room. "I personally requested him. I'm looking forward to his input."

Shayne raised his eyebrows. How did Hereth even know he existed? "Thank you, I'll do my best to…" He had no clue what he would be doing on the Council. "Uh, to do my best." He flashed a lame smile and felt his ears burn.

The Senior Council Member nodded. "The first order of business will be to hear from Council Member Yogath. He will present a brief update on the war."

Everyone opened their briefcases and pulled out file folders. Shayne had no file folders, so he glanced over the shoulder of the Council Member sitting next to him and folded his hands on the table.

Yogath, an old wrinkly fellow sitting on Hereth's right hand, spoke. "As of this morning, two more Dyken ships have been apprehended. Fifteen more have landed and since disappeared. This puts the total at three hundred eleven known landings."

A shiver of fear ran down Shayne's back. He had no idea that many Dyken ships came to Maslonia.

"As for the missing, we have an official count of thirty-seven thousand, four hundred sixty-five." Murmurs broke out and several people shifted in their chairs.

Hereth frowned. "What has been the outcome of the investigation on the missing?" He directed his question to a female sitting on his left.

She swallowed and looked down her long, pointy nose at her file. "We are certain they are being taken to a central location on Maslonia. Despite our best efforts, though, we have not been able to uncover it. We suspect a highly sophisticated cloaking system, similar to the one the Dykens use during abducting sprees. We know they are not being transported off-world. They are being kept here, alive. In fact, there is strong evidence to support the theory of memory alteration. Our people probably don't know they've been kidnapped." She tapped the end of her pencil on her paper. "The rest is mere speculation."

His mother was still here on this planet? Her memory…altered? Shayne's mind reeled. This must have been discussed before because no one else appeared shocked.

"What is the status of our troops, Cary?"

The gentleman sitting beside Shayne looked up. "We're taking heavy casualties. The more we send out, the more go missing. We're guarding every major threshold on the planet, but with dwindling resources, we're inevitably looking at a draft. Although with the rising numbers of missing…let's just say I've run the numbers and if abduction stints continue in the way they're going, we're looking at ten to twelve months before total annihilation."

Shayne sat through the rest of the meeting in stunned silence. Talk of evacuation plans and last resort weaponry were thrown around. In the end, they reluctantly agreed that retreating into the northern caves might be the best plan for those who were left when the time came.

After the meeting, Senior Council Member Hereth pulled Shayne aside in the hallway. The familiar gentle tugging sensation on his mind told him Hereth needed to speak to him privately.

I have a special task for you. Council Member Omar had been working on a way to contact those who have been abducted. I believe his progress in this project was the reason he was taken last week. I've heard of your abilities. I think your mind might be strong enough to continue on with his work.

Hereth pulled out a thick file and handed it to Shayne.

I'll do whatever I can, Shayne thought.

Everything you'll need should be in here. I didn't want to mention it in front of anyone, just in case. Hereth's eyes darkened.

Shayne took in a breath. *You think there is a mole among us?*

Hereth gave Shayne a hard look. *I* know *there is.*

Shayne's mouth went dry. He clutched the file closer and gave Hereth a parting nod.

The second sun hung low in the sky, and Shayne knew it would soon become chilly. He walked over to his car and reached into his pocket. It was empty.

Leaning over, he peered into the driver's side window. His keys hung from the ignition. Mentally kicking himself, he concentrated on the lock, feeling it with his mind. One gentle shove and the lock popped up.

"That was good."

"What?" Shayne spun around.

A man in a Council uniform stood several feet from him. He had a small build, but something about him seemed impressive. Shayne guessed he was about his mother's age. "What you did with that lock. Very impressive. Now there are three of us on the Council with telekinetic abilities. Of course, some of the other powers are helpful, but I think Hereth finds telekinesis appealing since it's his own power as well." He stuck his briefcase under his arm and extended his hand. "The name's Trenton. Trenton Madison."

Shayne took the man's hand. "Shayne Bartlet."

"Yes." Trenton smiled, the lines around his eyes crinkling. "Hereth speaks quite highly of you."

Shayne didn't know what to say, so he mumbled, "Thank you." That sounded stupid. He glanced around for something else to say. "Nice day today."

Trenton looked at the sky and nodded. "I heard Hereth gave you Omar's file."

An uncomfortable feeling tingled in his spine. "I, uh…" He didn't want to confirm this information, after what Hereth had said, so he glanced around again.

"Hey, it's okay, Hereth told me. I know he's a bit paranoid, but you'll get used to it." Trenton brushed a strand of black hair from his forehead.

"Do you really think there is a mole among us?" he blurted out.

Trenton seemed to size him up with a glance. "I don't know. Some pretty strange coincidences have happened since the first attack." He shrugged. "It's possible, I guess. The Dyken technology is also highly advanced. They could be getting all of their information on their own."

Shayne nodded, not sure of what else to say.

"Well, I just came over to wish you luck with Omar's project and welcome you to the Council."

"Thanks."

Trenton turned and walked away. Shayne slid behind the wheel, throwing the file on the passenger seat. He took in a deep breath and started his car, a jet black thunderbolt. It wasn't the newest model, but he didn't care. His mother had saved for months to buy it for him. His throat constricted thinking of her.

Thoughts swirled around in his mind as he drove. Some came from people in the city, and he tried to tune them out. The people were scared. They should be. They were being abducted by the thousands and there was no way to stop it.

He pulled into his aunt's driveway. He still wasn't used to living there. The house was a bit too formal for him. At least his aunt gave him space. She'd be the last person to ask about his love life. Unlocking the front door, he entered the empty house. She wasn't due back from work for another hour.

Shayne turned on several lights in the living room before tossing the file on the coffee table. He'd read it tonight. Right now he didn't want to think about the Dykens or the war. He didn't feel like eating anything, but he went to the fridge and opened it.

The floorboards creaked behind him and he froze. Mentally, he reached out, feeling the space around him. Someone was there in the kitchen with him. Someone he couldn't see. A cloaked Dyken.

He tensed, feeling for movement and waiting for the right moment. He sensed the Dyken raise his arm and Shayne ducked as he mentally sent a jar of mayonnaise flying out of the fridge. A low thud sounded and he heard a gasp. The cloaked figure moved and Shayne turned, throwing himself into a forward roll, knocking the invisible Dyken down.

"Ouch," the Dyken called out, and it surprised him to hear it was female.

He stumbled into the living room, using his mind to send objects flying behind him as he went. Something must have come in contact with her cloaking device for the Dyken girl appeared and he spun around. She couldn't have been any older than him; her brown hair pulled back into a loose knot at the base of her neck. The smattering of freckles on her nose and cheeks gave her almost a child-like appearance. She was dressed in tight fitting black clothes with a belt carrying an assortment of gadgets snug on her waist. The shock at being uncloaked was apparent on her face.

She held out her hand, as if to stop him from moving. "It's okay. I'm not here to hurt you."

The sincerity in her voice surprised Shayne. She couldn't possibly mean what she said. He probed her mind, looking for her true intent. Trying to read her mind was like running through a deep pool of water. Not as easy as connecting with someone of his own race, but not impossible either. He got the gist of what she was thinking.

"You're here to kidnap me."

She frowned. "It's not what you think."

He stepped back, stunned as to what he heard from her thoughts. "You think what you're doing is somehow…helping us. How can that be?"

She took a step closer to him. "We *are* here to help. There's no need to worry."

"If your friends and family were disappearing in droves, wouldn't you worry? Wouldn't you do everything in your power to stop it?"

Sympathy filled her eyes. "Of course I would." She lowered her voice. "Unless…I understood the whole picture." She edged closer, her hand flexing to grab one of her gadgets.

His muscles tensed. That's when he saw it. Omar's file. It sat on the coffee table in plain sight.

Shoot.

He probed the kitchen, looking for a distraction. A drinking glass sat on the counter and he gave it a mental shove. The shattering glass startled her, and she turned her head. He nudged the file with his mind and it slid under the couch. Then he pounced, pushing her up against the wall and holding her arms so she couldn't reach her belt.

A gasp escaped her lips.

I can't believe he smells as good as he looks.

That was unexpected. He chuckled. He couldn't help it.

Her green eyes flashed at him. "This isn't funny. You're only making this more difficult for yourself."

Pressed against her, he could feel her heart hammering. Her thoughts jumbled and he couldn't get a clear reading from her.

"Why are you doing this?"

"Let me go." She didn't struggle against him. If anything, she relaxed a little.

"Tell me what's going on. Where are you taking my people? Where is my mother?"

She frowned. "We haven't hurt anyone. They're safe. We're not the bad guys here."

"You think *we're* the bad guys?" Realization shocked him. "Why? What have we ever done to you?"

Her eyes looked past him. She gave a slight nod, and his arms and legs tingled. His muscles became useless and he crumpled to the floor.

"What are you doing, Danielle? You weren't supposed to decloak," a male voice spoke behind him.

"It was an accident." She knelt over Shayne, fiddling with something on her belt. She touched it to the back of his neck, and all thought signatures were silenced. He was completely deaf.

He tried to speak, but his muscles wouldn't work. She pulled out another gadget and pressed it against his arm. "Don't worry, he'll forget all about this once…"

The room spun. Everything went black.

Chapter 2

Shayne rubbed the back of his neck. This test was more difficult than he thought it would be. He had heard Hereth was harder on his students than most teachers. Unfortunately, he couldn't get out of it. He needed the credits, and this western civilization class was the only one that worked in his schedule.

After finishing the exam, he stood up and stalked to the front of the room. He was the second to last one to place his paper on Hereth's desk and leave.

The afternoon sunshine felt good when he got outside. Shayne stretched and took in a deep breath. He plopped his books on the grass and sat. Biology class wasn't for another fifty minutes. Scanning the boarding school campus, he looked at the stone buildings. He was lucky to be here at one of the finest college prep boarding schools in the

United States. Similar to a college campus, the school's only difference was the strict curfew and rules for the students.

Most of the students here had gotten in because of their parents' financial status. Shayne, on the other hand, had no family money. His academics had gotten him accepted, which meant he had to work twice as hard as the others in order to stay enrolled.

As he watched the students coming and going, a nagging feeling tugged at the back of his mind. Something important lay beneath the surface, but he couldn't grasp it. He shrugged. If it was critical, he would eventually remember it.

***

Trenton Madison walked down the corridor, passing the conference rooms on the left and the portals into the Holodome on the right. The corridor had a slight curve to it, following the perimeter of the Holodome. The white walls gave him the sterile feeling of a hospital or nursing home. Lights suspended in mid-air above him kept the corridor bright and emitted a quiet buzzing sound.

General Stott came out of his office and stopped Trenton. "I wanted to let you know we successfully integrated the rest of Johnstown into the Holodome thanks to your help. The memory resequencing has been going smoothly. No one suspects they're not really from twenty-first century Earth."

Trenton let the satisfaction wash over him. "And have you implemented my suggestions for those living in the northern hills?"

The Dyken General nodded. Everything about General Stott was crisp from his clean haircut to his neatly pressed uniform. Even his five o'clock shadow seemed somehow orderly, as if his hair wouldn't grow unless given permission. "Yes. We can start the mining process soon."

"I expect to be informed before the mining begins. I've decided I want half my payment up front."

General Stott narrowed his eyes. "You'll get your payment as agreed upon."

Trenton's anger flared. "I've practically handed over the entire planet for your taking. Without me, none of this would have been possible." Trenton concentrated all his mental abilities on the General's chest. He reached out with his mind, speeding up the molecules in Stott's heart.

The General's eyes widened. "What are you doing?" He threw his arm out and caught Trenton's throat, pushing him against the wall. "Stop that," he said between clenched teeth.

Trenton eased off, gasping for breath.

General Stott's face grew red and he pressed harder. "You forget, Maslonian, that you gave us the key to disabling your little powers. Try that again and I'll have you declawed."

Trenton waited for the General to let him go. Then he smoothed his shirt down and smiled. "I may have helped you, but I haven't left my people defenseless."

"What are you implying?"

Trenton smirked. "You still need me. I want half my payment up front or you'll be dealing with a bunch of telepaths who have discovered they can do more than read minds. And then your nicely laid plan will fail."

The Dyken General clenched his jaw, and his face turned a deeper red. "Don't threaten me, Maslonian."

"I wouldn't dream of threatening you, General." Trenton listened, probing the General's mind. Getting thoughts from a Dyken proved to be difficult for him, but sometimes he could catch a feeling if he concentrated. What he felt from Stott was fear. He pressed on. "Half my payment. In one week."

"I'll see what I can do." General Stott turned on his heel and left Trenton standing in the hall.

***

"Hey girlfriend, what'cha readin'?"

Danielle Darmok smiled, but didn't look up from her novel as Jennaya plunked beside her on the bench overlooking the campus. When she volunteered to remain on Maslonia to help out in the Holodome, she didn't expect to work so closely with the people. She found herself growing fond of them. Leaving in a few weeks might prove to be difficult for her.

"A book," she said, knowing it would bug Jennaya.

Jennaya squirmed. "Duh. I guess the more important question would be *why* are you reading? It's such a nice day out here and there are so many good looking guys running around the campus."

Danielle kept reading, even though the smile grew on her face. "There's a good looking guy in here too."

Jennaya hopped off the bench and snatched the book.

"Hey!"

"Guys on paper don't even compare to real life guys." Jennaya kept her short black hair cropped in a trendy style, matching her cute tank top and stylish shorts. Her eyes twinkled, daring Danielle to try to get her novel back.

Danielle jumped and swiped at the book, missing it by inches. Jennaya let out a screech and ran, her sandals slapping the sidewalk. Danielle scrambled after her.

"Jen! Give me that." Danielle's short legs were no match for Jennaya's long ones. Jennaya took off around the back side of the science hall. By the time Danielle caught up with her, Jennaya stood on the edge of the large circular water fountain in the center of campus.

"Come on, Danielle, say you'll go do something with me." Jennaya walked backwards along the fountain wall, Danielle's novel hanging precariously over the water. "You don't want your book to get wet."

"Hey, that's not funny. I was just at the good part." Danielle chewed her lip, trying to decide when to strike. Jennaya paused for a second, and Danielle jumped on the edge of the fountain. The sudden movement startled Jennaya, and she yanked her arm back. Danielle overshot her distance, and one foot slipped off the edge, leaving her teetering and flapping her arms about. She braced herself for the cold as she fell into the fountain. She gasped and let out a funny, high pitched sound as the water splashed over her.

She looked up and noticed Jennaya had dropped the book on the grass and was creeping down from the ledge, her mouth in the shape of an 'o'.

"Oh, no, you don't." Danielle reached out and yanked on Jennaya's arm, drawing her into the fountain as well.

The girls were dripping wet, giggling and carrying their shoes when they saw someone on the grass. It looked as though he were relaxing and studying the clouds, however as they neared him, they could tell he had fallen asleep. His blonde hair was spiked and bleached on the tips, and the hot sun was leaving its mark on his fair skin.

"You should wake him up," Jennaya said.

Danielle frowned. "Me?"

"He's more your type."

Danielle peered over at him. "He is cute." Then recognition hit her and her stomach tightened. It's him. The one she almost let get away. Shayne Bartlet. He would have ruined everything for her.

She edged a little closer to him, suddenly nervous but not sure why. He wouldn't recognize her. They wouldn't have placed him in the Holodome unless his memory resequencing had been successful.

Jennaya gave her a shove. "Go on."

"All right. Stop pushing." Danielle glared at Jennaya before walking up the gentle slope of grass to where he lay. She cleared her throat.

***

Shayne felt something wet fall on his face. He looked up. There was a girl in the sky with long brown hair dripping on him.

"Excuse me," she said.

The hazy feeling of sleep drifted from him, and he shook his head, sitting up.

"You, uh, fell asleep in the sun."

"What? Oh my goodness!" Shayne shot to his feet. "What time is it?" He felt the tight skin on his face.

The girl looked at her watch. "Four-thirty."

"Oh no, I've missed my biology class!" Frantic, he started gathering his books. He stopped and looked up, noticing the other girl on the sidewalk. "Has it been raining?" Even as the words left his lips, he knew they were idiotic, for he was quite dry except for the few drops of water still on his face.

"No," the two girls said in unison, water dripping from their soaked clothes and hair.

"Oh. Of course not." He picked up his books and turned, feeling like he was missing something obvious.

"Bye," the girl with the brown hair called.

Shayne smiled and held up his hand in a half-hearted wave. The girls continued down the sidewalk, chatting with each other. He stared after them, wondering why he couldn't look away.

***

Shayne pushed his shopping cart down the snack food aisle. Soft rock played over the speakers as he tried to decide if he wanted plain or rippled chips. There were advantages to being a senior, and getting to live in the apartment style dorms was the best one. He didn't have to eat in the disgusting cafeteria if he didn't want to.

After staring at the selection for what seemed to be an inordinate amount of time, he finally snapped out of it and grabbed a bag. A couple of younger girls pushed past him, giggling about who knows what.

The girl that woke him up from his nap yesterday walked past his aisle, a small shopping basket hung on her arm. She wore Capri style pants with a plain white t-shirt, her brown hair pulled up into a simple ponytail. Something about her bugged him, but he couldn't quite put his finger on it.

He steered his shopping cart down the aisle and turned in her direction. She wasn't there. Scanning the aisles as he walked, he figured she couldn't have gone far. He got to the end of the market before spying her in the frozen foods section.

He wheeled his shopping cart and stopped right beside her, not really knowing what he was going to say. She glanced at him and smiled.

"Hi," he said, realizing he didn't even know her name. "It's…you." A sheepish grin crept onto his face.

"Yes, it is." She peered at him.

"I, um…" He searched for something great to say. Inspiration hit him. "I wanted to thank you for saving me from a terrible sunburn yesterday."

"You're welcome." The girl smiled.

He stuck out his hand. "I'm Shayne."

"Danielle." She brushed an invisible strand of hair from her eyes and took his outstretched hand. A thin gold ring on her right hand caught his eye. He liked her simple tastes.

"You're shopping?" He mentally slapped his hand to his head. What a dumb question.

"Yes. I was just trying to decide on a vegetable to go with dinner." She scanned the frozen foods, a slight frown on her face.

"Well now, let's see." Shayne rubbed his chin in mock concentration. "If you're having chicken, then I would suggest broccoli. However, beef lends itself more toward the corn or carrot variety."

She squinted at him for a second. "What goes with rabbit?"

He resisted the urge to laugh. She was pulling his leg of course, but something told him to keep a straight face. He searched for something to say. "That depends. Is it a large jackrabbit, or a small baby bunny?"

A smile played on her lips. "I'm not sure. I found it on the side of the road."

Shayne couldn't stop himself; he let out a chuckle, and Danielle smirked. "Made you laugh," she said.

"I think you cheated." Shayne raised one eyebrow.

Danielle reached for a package of frozen peas. "I don't cheat." She flashed a grin at him. "I'd better be going or my roommate will eat without me and the vegetables."

Shayne wanted to say something to make her stay, but couldn't think of anything. "Well, enjoy your bunny." Several people turned and gave him strange looks.

He watched her as she moved toward the check out aisle, a twinge of disappointment nudging him. Had she been flirting with him, or just making polite conversation? He wasn't sure, but he resolved to find out.

***

Danielle clutched the bag of groceries as she entered her dorm room. Jennaya, sprawled out on the couch, looked up from her magazine. "That took longer than I thought. Were you growing your own vegetables?"

"Ha, funny. No, I ran into someone at the market." Danielle set the grocery bag down on the counter and started taking things out.

"Really? Who?"

"That guy we woke up yesterday."

Jennaya stood and tossed her magazine down. "The cute one? Oooh, girl, tell all."

The pots clanged as Danielle searched for one to steam the peas in. "Well, his name is Shayne."

"Shayne!" Jennaya clasped her hands together. "Great name. What else?"

Danielle turned the faucet on, running water into the pan before speaking. "There's really nothing much else to tell. He ran into me at the store and said 'hi.' We chatted for a minute, and then I left."

"You just left him there?"

Danielle's hand flew to her mouth. "Oh my gosh, you're right. What was I thinking, leaving him in the grocery store? How will he ever survive?"

Frowning, Jennaya placed her hands on her hips. "That's not what I meant, goofball. Why didn't you ask him over? We have plenty of meatloaf."

Danielle hid a smile and turned back to the peas. The thought had crossed her mind, but she wasn't going to admit that to Jennaya. "Yeah, that sounds like something you would do."

Jennaya huffed, stomping into the living room only three steps away. She picked up her magazine, stomped over to the armchair, and sunk in it. "Fine, don't come out of your shell. Just let the world go by while you hide in your dorm room alone."

Danielle didn't answer, so Jennaya stuck her nose in the magazine, bouncing her leg. After a few minutes she slapped the magazine down on the end table and went back into the kitchen. "You'd never ask him over?"

She opened the cupboard, handing Jennaya two plates and two mugs. "Why don't you ask him, if you're so interested?"

"Maybe I will." Jennaya set the dishes on the small kitchen table, coming back for the silverware. "He is cute."

"Yes. He's cute." The look on Shayne's face when she said she was cooking a rabbit made her snicker.

"What?"

"Well, we were joking about what we were going to eat for dinner. I told him we were going to have rabbit." She laughed.

Jennaya made a face. "Gross."

That made Danielle laugh even harder. "I guess you had to be there."

"I guess so."

After dinner Danielle said something about having to study and shut herself up in her room. She knew Jennaya wouldn't bother her, so she slid into her computer chair and wiggled her mouse. While she had a chance, she'd better log in and give her update.

A twinge of guilt spread over her. She pushed it away. She knew this was necessary.

The computer screen came to life and a blue desktop appeared. She clicked on the small world icon in the bottom left corner entitled Project Earth. A user name and password screen came up.

She typed Dyken1478 for her username and supplied her authentication password. The desktop disappeared leaving the cursor blinking in the upper left corner of a blank screen.

She typed: *All is going as planned. Created memories are intact. No sign of extra abilities have surfaced. I will check in next week unless something comes up. Dyken1478.*

As soon as she hit enter her words disappeared from the screen. The cursor sat and blinked for a while. Then these words appeared: *Update accepted. No new instructions available for Dyken1478.*

She hit enter again, and the screen returned to the desktop.

Chapter 3

Nolen took his daughter's hand and shifted the large pack on his shoulders. "I'm sorry, honey, we have to keep going."

Gita's black eyes gazed up at him; her little pink backpack bobbing as she walked, sweat glistening on her dark skin. "But I'm tired." Disappointment crept onto her face, and a little guilt wormed its way into his heart.

"Maybe we can stop and rest in a few minutes," Celeste said, looking over her shoulder at them.

Nolen nodded, appreciative of the way his wife knew how to smooth things over. Tall and thin with creamy milk chocolate skin and high cheek bones, she looked every bit as young as when he married her. He worried about what this would do to her…to all of them.

He continued to follow Celeste up the steep, rocky mountain side. "The larger sun is low in the sky. We have about four more hours until darkness falls."

"Daddy, I don't want to be out here in the dark. I want to go home."

"I know, sweetheart. But we can't go home, remember? The bad people will find us. We have to find a place to hide."

Celeste shot him a warning glance. "It will be an adventure," his wife said, smiling. "We'll be camping."

"I've never been camping," Gita said.

"See, we'll be trying something new." Celeste hitched her pack up. "And I heard these caves are beautiful."

"Are there bats?"

Celeste shook her head. "I don't think so, honey."

Nolen's boot snagged a tree root and he fell, his hand hitting a jagged rock. Pain shot up his arm, and blood dripped down his fingers.

"Daddy! You're hurt." She squatted down beside him, taking his hand in hers. *Hold still, Daddy.* Placing her palm on the cut, her eyebrows knit together in concentration. Warmth surged through his hand. The pain stopped. When she removed her hand the gash was gone.

"Thank you, my little one."

***

The Overtaking

It had been a week since Shayne ran into Danielle in the grocery store. He'd been trying to catch a glimpse of her as he walked to and from classes, but hadn't been successful. Until now. When he saw her, his chest constricted and his breath caught in his lungs. She was walking up the slight incline toward the south end of campus, hugging her books to her chest. He picked up his pace in order to join her.

Falling into step beside her, he said, "Hi."

Her head jerked up at the sound of his voice. "Oh, hello."

Surprise showed on her face, but was that a hint of pleasure as well? Shayne wasn't sure. "How was your meal? I never did find out what you were really having."

The fall breeze blew a few loose strands of her hair from her ponytail, and she brushed them aside. "Meatloaf. And it was delicious, thank you."

"I should have you over for dinner. I'm not a bad cook myself. I'm far better than my mother ever was." Where did that come from? His mother died when he was a child. He could hardly remember anything about her.

"Are you asking me out on a date?" This must have pleased her because her lips turned up into a smile.

"I don't know if out is the proper term for a home cooked meal. I guess I'm asking you in on a date."

Her smile widened. "Well, then, I accept. Where do you live?"

"I'm in the dorm rooms over on Fifth Street. Apartment twelve."

She raised her eyebrow. "Will we be dining alone?"

"No, I live with my…roommate. I'm sure he'll be there." What was wrong with him? He was about to say he lived with his mother. How absurd. He shook it off. "How about coming over about six tonight? I'll make you my famous chicken cordon bleu."

"Mmm, sounds delicious, and it will be nice to meet your roommate too. Well, here's my building. Thank you for inviting me over. I'll see you tonight."

"See you." He pretended to tip a hat to her. She smiled and disappeared into the building.

Shayne turned and headed back the other way. A strange feeling overcame him. What was up with all that about his mother?

***

After picking up a few needed ingredients at the store, Shayne headed to his dorm. He opened the door and called out, "Mom, I'm…" A sick feeling started in the pit of his stomach. He hadn't grown up with his mother, and yet he knew he had lived with her until a short time ago. The familiarity of it was too strong.

He walked into the kitchen and closed his eyes. Yes. He could see her face now. Her favorite flowers were violets. When he was sixteen, she taught him how to drive. She would always sing him to sleep as a child.

A stabbing pain seared through his head, and he doubled over. Something wet trickled down his face. A bloody nose. He grabbed a tissue from the counter and leaned over the sink.

What was going on? He never knew his mother. The funeral had been held on a rainy day in September when he was just a child. He remembered the way his aunt had sobbed, and then moving in with her and his uncle in New Hampshire.

He wiped at his nose and shook his head. Mental illness must run in his family. The front door opened and his roommate Brady walked in.

He took one look at him and balked. "You okay?"

"Just a nosebleed."

Brady frowned. "Well, you're bleeding all over the floor."

Shayne made a face. "Sorry, next time I'll defy gravity and bleed on the ceiling."

"You're so funny I actually thought about laughing that time." Brady hooked his thumbs in his pockets and rocked back on his heels. "What are you making?"

"Chicken cordon bleu."

He raised his eyebrows. "What's the occasion?"

Shayne pulled the tissue away from his face to see if it had stopped bleeding. "I finally met up with Danielle today and invited her over for dinner."

"Dude." He stretched it out into two syllables. "Way to go. Do you need any help?"

"No offense, but I've eaten your cooking. I think I'll be fine on my own." He turned on the faucet and stuck his hands under the running water.

Acting like a knife had been plunged into his chest, Brady staggered back. "Ouch, man, that hurt."

"I said, 'no offense.'"

"So, you can insult me as long as you say 'no offense' first?"

"Yep." Shayne flashed a huge grin at him. Before he knew it, Brady had grabbed the faucet, squirting water in his face. "Hey, I've got a date tonight!" Shayne laughed as he shut off the faucet.

Brady balled up a fist and tapped him on the shoulder. "You want me to make myself scarce tonight, so you can have some alone time with her?"

"No, don't leave. Why don't you join us for dinner? I get the feeling it might make her uncomfortable if you're not around."

A smile lit up Brady's round face. "Sure thing. I can hang around, eat your food, and flirt with your girl."

"No flirting allowed, or I'll throw you out on your ear."

***

The evening sun hung low while white puffs of clouds drifted across the sky. The trees swayed in the gentle breeze. Danielle sighed. It reminded her of home, and a wave of nostalgia washed over her. She tried to push it out of her head.

She climbed the steps to apartment twelve and knocked on the door. Shayne swung the door open. He smiled when he saw her, and her stomach fluttered. The way he looked at her made her knees go weak.

"Hi. Come on in," he said.

"Thanks. I brought you something." She held out a bottle of sparkling grape juice.

"Wonderful. I'll get out my special plastic cups." He stepped aside to let her in.

"What, no stemware?" The warm aromas of the kitchen greeted her as she walked inside.

"I keep my fancy dishes in my mansion." He shut the door and motioned to a guy with dark hair and muscular arms sitting on an orange loveseat. "Danielle, this is my roommate Brady."

"Nice to meet you." Brady stood and held out his hand.

He wore a thin gold ring on the middle finger of his right hand. A Dyken. She smiled and shook his hand. He threw her a questioning look before smoothing out his features.

"Glad to meet you, Brady."

Shayne held up the bottle. "I'll go put this in the kitchen."

The cramped living room connected to the kitchen. The carpet ended abruptly, turning into linoleum. A small table sat pushed against the wall beside the refrigerator. Once he was out of earshot,

Brady whispered, "You surprised me. I thought he was gaga over a Maslonian girl."

The flutters intensified. "He's gaga over me?"

Brady laughed. "Yeah."

Shayne wandered into the room. "Well, it's about ready if you want to come into the kitchen. Sorry, the table is a little small for three, but I think we can make it work." They went into the kitchen and Shayne pulled out a chair, motioning for Danielle to sit.

Brady sat across from her while Shayne started dishing out the food.

"This smells delicious," she said.

"Thanks." Shayne grinned.

Brady picked up a fork. "Shayne's quite the cook. We've been in school less than a month and already I've gained five pounds." He patted his belly. "I think I'm getting spoiled."

Shayne shrugged and sat down on the end. "I enjoy it."

"Where did you learn to cook?" she asked.

"I'm self-taught. I had to either learn to cook or eat my mother's interesting creations." Shayne winced and shook his head.

A look crossed Brady's face, and he threw Danielle a worried glance. "I thought you were raised by your aunt."

Shayne nodded, fussing with his silverware. "Yeah, I meant to say my aunt." He flashed a smile at Danielle. "I guess I've been studying too hard. I can hardly remember my own name."

Brady laughed a little too loudly. "I know what you mean, bro. After we eat I've got to hit the books myself."

The conversation took a turn toward school, and they discussed their classes as they ate. Danielle watched Shayne closely, looking for signs of trouble. Something was wrong with his created memories, but she wasn't sure what. Usually the created memories were as similar as they could get to real memories, just changing little bits and pieces to fit their needs. She had no idea why they would change something as drastic as growing up with an aunt instead of his mother. There would have been no need.

"So, Danielle, what do you want to do after you graduate?" Shayne asked.

"I'm applying to K State to get a communications degree. I'd like to go into public relations."

"Ah, you want to become a spin doctor."

Danielle picked up her fork. "Be nice, I've got a weapon."

After they finished eating, Shayne excused himself to use the bathroom. Danielle picked up her plate and took it over to the sink, Brady following close behind. She whispered, "What was that about his mother?"

Brady's eyebrows pulled together. "I'm not sure. He's not supposed to remember his mother. Could have just been a slip of the tongue. It hasn't happened before now."

A twinge of worry crept over Danielle. "Actually, I'm pretty sure he mentioned his mother to me earlier today." She turned on the faucet and stopped up the sink. "Why didn't they station him with his family anyway? Usually they keep family together."

Brady frowned. "I don't know. All I was told is that something happened and they had to create more extensive memories for him and to watch him closely. I'm going to have to report this. Apparently, he's got stronger powers than most."

"Yes, he's a telekinetic," she said, thinking of the day she was sent to take him. They hadn't warned her in advance. It might not have helped anyway. All rational thought had left her when she saw him. He was so good looking all she could do was stare. It was like he had stepped off a movie screen. If she hadn't been so distracted, he never would have seen her face. Not that it mattered now. Those memories were erased. At least, they were supposed to be.

"I think his mind-reading powers are more powerful too." Brady gathered the plastic cups from the table while Danielle squirted some dish washing solution into the sink. Bubbles formed under the running water. "But I haven't seen any resurfacing of those."

"That's good."

"What's good?" Shayne asked.

Danielle turned with a start, slopping dish water onto the floor. "Oh, you startled me."

"Sorry." He ripped off a paper towel and mopped up the mess.

Her hands trembled, so she stuck them into the soapy water. "That's okay. We were just talking about how good your meal was."

Shayne smiled. "I'm glad you liked it." He opened a drawer and took out a dishtowel. "Next time I'll take you out to eat. Do you like Chinese?"

Danielle couldn't tell if she were more pleased he hadn't heard them talking, or that he was asking her out again. "I do."

Brady threw her a look that she interpreted as 'be careful.' "Well, I'm going to go hit the books."

"Okay." Shayne turned to take a plate from her. "See ya."

Brady ducked out of the room.

"He's nice," she said, trying to make polite conversation.

"Yes, he's a good roommate. Doesn't play his music loud or anything. We get along okay."

"That's good." She scrubbed at a plate with a washrag, and then ran it under the water. When Shayne reached for it, their fingers touched, sending sparks through her hand. She tried to breathe normally.

"Did you grow up around here?"

"No, I'm from Washington state, but my Dad went to this boarding school, and he thought it would build character," she lied.

He nodded. "I grew up in New Hampshire. It will be interesting spending this winter here in Kansas. I'm not sure what to expect."

She smiled feebly. She had no idea what kind of winters Kansas had. She decided to change the subject. "I saw your western civilization book. Which teacher do you have?"

Shayne made a face. "Hereth."

"Oh, I heard he was tough."

"That's an understatement."

They talked about their different teachers as they finished up with the dishes. Once they were put away, Shayne motioned toward the living room. "Do you want to sit a while?"

Heck yes. But she knew she should get back to her dorm room. She was supposed to be keeping an eye on Jennaya and the other girls in the complex. "Actually, I'd better get going. I've got a huge test tomorrow."

Disappointment flickered briefly across his face, and then he smiled. "Would you like me to walk you home?"

Her heart sped up. "Sure."

Brady came out of his bedroom. He threw her a meaningful glance as he walked by.

"I'm going to walk Danielle home. I'll be right back," Shayne said.

"Okay." Brady grabbed a cup and stuck it under the faucet. "I'll be here."

Danielle headed with Shayne to the door. As they stepped outside, a sky streaked with orange and pink clouds greeted them. "What a beautiful sunset."

"I guess I'm surrounded by beauty then," he said, winking at her.

Danielle felt her cheeks grow hot. She concentrated on breathing in and out as they advanced down the sidewalk.

When they got to the street, Shayne slowed. "Which dorms are you in?"

"The ones on First and Ash. It's faster to cut across campus." Why did her voice have to sound so breathy?

Shayne followed her lead and they crossed the street toward the school. Once they were on campus, he slipped his hand in hers. Warmth spread through her, and she smiled up at him.

By the time they stood in front of her building, the sun sank below the horizon. He turned to face her. The soft light of dusk lit up his eyes. "This it?"

"Yes." She didn't let go of his hand. She never wanted to let go of his hand.

He reached out with his other hand and gently caressed her face with the back of his fingers. Before she could stop herself, she stood on her toes and brushed her lips against his. He responded by pulling her close, pressing his lips more firmly on hers. She instinctively entwined her fingers in his hair. The world began to spin and she wondered if she was going to pass out. She didn't mind as long as he held her.

A familiar low hum buzzed behind her, and she broke away, breathless. A bright rectangle of light appeared, and several Dyken men dressed in black came through the portal. *They're here to take Shayne.* Her heart jumped into her throat.

Shayne gasped. "What the–"

They rushed at him, knocking him down, almost taking her with them.

Danielle screamed, "What are you doing? He's not armed."

They scuffled with Shayne on the cement. "Danielle, run!"

She stood there, frozen. They handcuffed him and jerked him to his feet. A trickle of blood oozed from his forehead. He continued to struggle against them until one of the Dykens injected him with a neural inhibitor. His head sagged. The men held him under his arms so he didn't hit the pavement.

The tall one turned to Danielle. "He's to be taken to a debriefing room along with you." He fiddled with the ring on his middle finger, reopening the portal. "You'll need to come with us."

She nodded. The men half-carried, half-dragged Shayne's lax body into the portal.

Danielle waited until she couldn't see their dark shapes on the other side. Then she stepped through, the decompressing sensation taking her breath away for a second. The bright corridor lights made her squint. The portal hummed behind her, and she pressed the red button on the wall beside it so it would close.

The Overtaking

Her throat constricted, and she steeled herself for what was going to come next.

Chapter 4

Nolan awoke to a rustling noise outside the cave. Celeste stirred in the sleeping bag next to him. "Shh, I think I hear something," he whispered.

She sat up. "An animal?"

"Could be." The pale moonlight shone outside, casting dark shadows. He raised his hand, palm up, and willed the fire to come. A flame burst forth and sat on his palm. He peered around the cave and out into the darkness. No movement.

"Maybe it was my imagination." He extinguished the fire and his wife lay back down.

"If it's a rabbit, catch it for breakfast."

"The last rabbit I shot, Gita healed." He grinned in the darkness.

"Her stomach will get the better of her eventually. We can't eat berries forever, and there won't be any in the winter."

The winter. Nolan didn't want to think about that. Sleeping a few feet into the cave was fine for now; the nights weren't cold. But soon the bitter wind would force them to crawl back into the deeper recesses. Gita wouldn't like that.

Another rustle sounded, and a raccoon stuck its nose into the cave, sniffing. "Celeste, it's a raccoon."

"Do those taste good?" Celeste mumbled.

"I don't know. I can't kill it now. It will wake Gita."

Celeste whispered something incoherent and rolled over. The raccoon stood on its haunches, his red eyes staring at Nolan. Soft snoring sounds came from Celeste.

A branch snapped and the raccoon bolted into the cave, past their sleeping bags and disappeared into the dark.

Nolan was about to create more light when a dark figure stumbled into the mouth of the cave. He staggered and fell, crumpling to the ground.

Nolan's heart thumped. He scrambled out of his sleeping bag and rushed over to the man. He was dressed in black. A Dyken. Crusty blood covered half of his face.

"Celeste! Come here."

His wife shot to her feet and rushed over to him. "We've been found," she said, clutching at her nightshirt, her eyes staring out into the night.

"No. Look at him. He's injured. I don't think he knew we were in this cave."

Celeste examined the man's bloody face. "Perhaps. But there could be more of them."

Nolan rolled the man onto his back. His belt held several gadgets that looked ominous to Nolan. They could be weapons. He pulled them off and handed them to his wife. "Put these somewhere safe."

With a nod, Celeste took them and went to the back of the cave, putting them in her pack.

"Bring me a rope," Nolan said, half-whispering.

He heard rummaging, and then his wife reappeared. "What are you going to do?" Celeste asked, handing him the coil of white rope.

"I'm going to tie him up."

"What if others come looking for him?" Fear darkened her brown eyes.

"Then we'll deal with it. I have a gun, and plenty of ammo. I'll stay up and watch the cave while you sleep." Nolan brought the man's hands together and wrapped the rope around his wrists, securing it with a tight knot. One of his swollen fingers held a thin gold band, and Nolan wondered if that was a wedding ring. The man groaned, but did not wake.

"After I tie his ankles, find his injury and heal it."

His wife gasped. "I'm not going to heal him."

"He could die."

"Our people have been hunted down and kidnapped. They've taken all of our loved ones. Our friends. And you worry about the death of one of *them*?"

Nolan finished tying the knot securing the man's feet together. He scooted over and pulled Celeste's hands into his, the warmth of her skin causing his heart to race. "Dearest, I will not let this man hurt our family, and I will do whatever is necessary to protect us. But you are a healer. If you let this man die tied up on the floor of our cave, you will not be able to forgive yourself. I know you too well."

Moonlight bounced off her face, and her eyes traveled down to the man. "I can't heal someone who destroyed my life."

"Then it is you who needs healing, my love."

***

The throbbing sensation in his head woke Shayne. Where was he? He opened his eyes and squinted against the bright light. He felt something wet and warm trickling down his face and he reached up to touch it.

Blood.

He sat up and looked around. Four white walls stared back at him. He struggled to remember what had happened.

The men had kidnapped him and Danielle.

"Danielle!" His voice echoed through the small room. Where had they taken him?

He rubbed at his wrists where the handcuffs had bitten into him. Someone had taken them off.

Bracing against the wall, he stood. Fear worked its way down his spine.

How had he gotten in here? There were no windows or doors. He felt along the wall. There must be a trap door somewhere. He searched for crevices. Finding none, he turned to go to the opposite side of the room. An invisible force sent him bouncing backward.

What was *that*?

Putting his hands out in front of him, he felt a slight pressure. The harder he pressed, the stronger the force pushed back. He followed it and found the field divided the room in half.

A cold feeling settled in his stomach. "Where am I?" Maybe someone would hear him. "What have you done with Danielle?"

He paced back and forth along the invisible force. A rectangle on the far wall shimmered and vanished, and a man stepped through. The wall reappeared. Shayne stopped and faced the man, his muscles readying for a fight.

The man stood about a foot from Shayne with his hands behind his back. His jet black hair fell to his forehead in stark contrast to his smooth light skin. Even though he was slight, his authoritative presence filled the room. He didn't say a word, his dark, deep-set eyes penetrating through Shayne.

Shayne stared back at him, unable to break the silence. Finally the man's face softened. "Please relax. We wish you no harm."

His voice broke the spell. "Where is Danielle? What have you done with her?"

The man raised his eyebrows. "Danielle is fine," he said, his voice smooth. "She's in the other room. Try to calm down."

Calming down was the last thing on Shayne's mind. "I demand to see her. Let me out of here." He pushed against the force, unable to budge it.

The man frowned. "My name is Trenton. I need to ask you some questions."

Anger boiled deep inside of Shayne. "I won't answer any questions until I know Danielle is safe."

Trenton sighed. "That's fine. You don't need to speak. I just want you to listen. Think for a moment about your mother."

What?

"My mother? What are you talking about? Where is Danielle? What have you done to her?"

Trenton's frown deepened. "What comes to mind when I ask about your mother?"

Shayne scowled. This guy was crazy. "I'm not going to talk about my mother. I want to see Danielle."

For a moment Shayne thought the man was going to punch him, but he doubted Trenton could get through the invisible force any better than he could. A vein stood out on Trenton's neck and his face turned pink.

"You will see Danielle if you cooperate."

Shayne folded his arms across his chest. He pinched his lips together, refusing to give anything to this man.

Trenton stared at him for a minute, and then he turned on his heel and pressed his palm against the wall. The doorway appeared and Trenton stepped out, the wall rematerializing after he left.

"I demand to see Danielle!" He wondered if anyone could hear him. The cold silence answered back.

***

Danielle sat at a sleek glass table, her elbows resting on the edge and her hands on either side of her face. General Stott sat on one side of her and Brady on the other. They watched Shayne in the next room through the transparent wall. He paced back and forth, pressing on the force shield every once in a while, trying to get out. The cut on his forehead started to clot, and dried blood streaked the side of his face.

Trenton stalked in and pulled out a chair on the opposite side of the table.

"Well, what did you find out?" General Stott asked.

"He's not thinking about anything but Ms. Darmok. I can't tell how many of his memories have been compromised. I don't know if he knows about Maslonia or his telekinetic abilities."

They all turned to look at Danielle. She felt her cheeks warm. "What should we do?"

"You're going to have to go in there and talk to him," Trenton said. "He thinks the both of you have been kidnapped. Play along. Get him to calm down and maybe I can get a fix on what he remembers."

A horrible feeling clenched her gut. "Okay." She couldn't exactly refuse. The rest of them continued to stare at her. She stood, her chair making a scraping noise on the cement floor. "I'll see what I can do."

She inched over to the door.

"You can't go in alone. I'll have to get the guards to take you in." Trenton pulled out his communicator and spoke into it. A few moments later two Dyken guards came in the room and took her arms. They looked like the same men who had taken Shayne. They escorted her out of the room, down the hall to the next room, and pressed on the metal sensor. The door dematerialized.

They shoved her inside, a little too roughly in her opinion. The wall reappeared behind them.

"Danielle!" Shayne pressed his hands against the force shield. "Are you all right?"

Danielle nodded. "I'm okay."

One of the guards walked over, waved his hand across the wall, and an access panel appeared. Punching a few buttons, he lowered the force shield. The other guard shoved her forward. Shayne caught her, pulling her close to him.

The guard engaged the shield once more, and they both left.

Shayne turned to her. "What did they do to you?"

Danielle bit her lower lip. "Nothing. I'm fine." She reached up and gently touched the cut on his head. He winced. "Are you okay? You're bleeding."

"It's not that bad," he said, hugging her again. She buried her face in his chest. He smelled of musk and fabric softener. He cleared his throat. "I was so worried about you. I didn't know what they would do to you."

A sinking feeling started in her chest. If he only knew she was one of them. She shook the thought from her head. She had a job to do. "Hey, it's okay. I'm fine."

Worry showed in his eyes. "What do you think they want from us?"

"I don't know." She stared up at him, trying to think of something to say. An idea popped into her head. "They kept asking me what I know about your mother."

His eyes widened. "They asked me about her too. What does my dead mother have to do with anything?"

"I have no idea. I never knew your mother." She paused, feeling a little guilty for leading him into this, but then continued. "What can you remember about her?"

"Not that much. She died when I was young." He paused and his eyes narrowed. "But something strange has been going on." Conflict showed on his face, as if he wasn't sure if he should tell her.

"What's been happening?"

"I've been having memories of her that aren't real," he whispered. "I know, it sounds insane, but I could have sworn that my mother taught me how to drive. Even though she died years before I turned sixteen." He searched her face. "Do you think I'm going crazy?"

She forced a smile. "No. I don't think you're going crazy. Unless you've discovered you can hear my thoughts, or move objects with your mind." She laughed nervously.

"What?" He raised his eyebrows, and then chuckled. "No, I can't read minds or fly, and spider webs don't come out of my hands."

Relief flooded through her. He hadn't discovered any of his latent powers. The memory resequencing should be easy, and he can be once again placed in the Holodome.

The door dematerialized and Trenton walked in. "Very nicely done, Ms. Darmok. I've got everything I need. Excellent work."

Chapter 5

Danielle's heart stopped and she felt mortified. She looked up at Shayne. For a split second he looked confused, then he stepped back, a mask of horror on his face.

"Danielle? What's going on?"

Trenton almost glowed with glee. "She's helped us out tremendously. I'm most impressed." He turned to face her. "At first I thought your fraternizing with him was brainless, but you've proven me wrong. Well done."

The look of horror on Shayne's face turned to disgust. Danielle's knees wobbled, and she felt like throwing up. "No, it's not like that."

He turned away, as if he couldn't stand to look at her. The guards came back into the room, one of them holding another neural inhibitor. As the one waved his hand over the panel, she could see Shayne tense, getting ready for it.

"No!" she yelled, but it was too late. The shield went down and Shayne pounced, knocking the guard down, the neural inhibitor flying across the floor.

Shayne punched the guard in the face. Trenton's hand shot out and the inhibitor sprang up to his grasp. Another guard jumped on top of Shayne, holding him down while Trenton injected him.

Her heart thumped against her chest, and she exhaled.

Trenton straightened, smoothing his shirt. "Take him to the resequencing room. I want to observe this myself." He turned and began walking out.

"Wait," she called.

He stopped and turned, staring at her for a moment. "You want to know why Shayne wasn't stationed with his mother as normal protocol. I'll tell you why. His mother died during the takeover. A dreadful accident that couldn't be avoided. But our last resequencing was too drastic, a mistake we will not repeat. Thank you for your help. Now you may return to your duties in the Holodome." He left, the guards dragging Shayne's limp body after him.

Danielle pressed a cold hand to her forehead. Shayne's mother was dead? How did that happen? No one was supposed to get hurt. Her chest felt hollow.

She exited the room, turning down the corridor toward the Holodome portals. The first three portals had Dykens standing in front of them, punching in coordinates into the display panels. She walked to the fourth portal and pressed her palm against the sensor. A green light moved over her hand, and the display lit up.

Dyken1478 type in your coordinates.

Her fingers flew over the panel as she punched in the numbers and hit enter.

Processing...coordinates accepted. Maslonians in vicinity, please wait.

She took a deep breath and let it out slowly. The red light above the portal blinked for a minute before turning green.

Portal ready. Please enter.

The portal hummed and she could see the silhouettes of the trees outside of her dorm building. She stepped through, the breath squeezing out of her lungs with the compression. A second later she was through and the portal closed behind her. It was dark outside, and Danielle wondered what time it was.

She yanked on her door and Jennaya hopped off the couch. "Oh my gosh! It's midnight, girl! I told the dorm mom you were already asleep when she came for curfew call. Thank goodness she didn't check this time, or you'd be in real trouble. Your date must have gone well!" She hopped around the living room like she'd had too much sugar. "What happened? Did he kiss you? Are you going out again? Spill it. I want all the details."

Danielle walked into the room and sat down on the couch, forcing herself to smile. "Well, first he cooked me dinner." She stalled, trying to come up with something to say about the evening.

"Yes. Was he a good cook?"

"Fantastic," she said, remembering the meal, which of course made her feel even worse. She swallowed, trying to forget the last hour.

Jennaya curled up on the chair. "And then what?"

"We did the dishes together."

A frown crossed Jennaya's face.

"I know, real sexy, but it was fun. He's a down to earth guy, and I like that about him. Some guys have to take you out to a fancy restaurant to impress you. Shayne's not like that. He's not afraid to be himself."

"Cool. Go on."

She thought about his offer to sit for a while. "Then we watched some TV."

"Did he hold your hand?"

Did he? Since she was making this part up as she went along, she could say yes, but she wanted to keep it as close to reality as she could. "No, not then, but he held my hand when he walked me home."

"That's very romantic." Jennaya wiggled her eyebrows up and down. "But you're not allowed to be in the boys dorms after nine. Didn't you get in trouble?"

Crud. She'd better think of something to say. "We left his dorm at nine. He wanted to walk through the park and talk. I didn't realize it had gotten so late. I guess I lost track of time."

"Ha, you sure did. So what happened after the park?"

Butterflies assaulted her stomach as she thought about what happened next. Should she confess to Jennaya she was the one who kissed him? Debating for a second, she finally decided to end the story how she would have wanted it to end. "We stopped outside of the dorms and stood holding hands for a few minutes. I told him I had a wonderful time, and he asked me if I wanted to go out again."

Jennaya made a high pitched noise, her lips pressed together, like she could hardly hold it in.

Danielle continued. "Then he leaned over and kissed me."

"Oh my gosh, he kissed you! Was it a long kiss, or just a peck? Is he a good kisser?"

"An excellent kisser, definitely," she said, remembering the way he pulled her close, his lips moving against her own. "And it was a sort-of long kiss." It would have been longer had they not been interrupted.

"When are you going out again?"

"We haven't made any definite plans." She realized she didn't even have his phone number. But she could stop by his place tomorrow. He should be back home by morning, she supposed.

"Ooh, girl, you've got yourself a man! Now I just need to find a juicy morsel and we can double date." She rubbed her hands together.

"Shayne's roommate is single, and he's hot. I can see if they're free tomorrow night."

"Count me in. Now, since you took forever getting home and I haven't been able to think about

anything else, I'm exhausted and must go to bed."
She stretched her arms.

Danielle laughed. Jennaya was such a drama
queen. But she was right. She had quite a report to
file before she could go to bed. "Good night."

She brushed her teeth and logged onto the
computer. After typing out her report, conveniently
leaving out the kiss, she waited for further
instructions. The cursor blinked for an eternity on
her screen. After what seemed like forever, words
appeared on her screen.

*Update accepted. Shayne Bartlet is
undergoing resequencing at this moment. He will
return to the Holodome before dawn. No new
instructions for Dyken1478.*

She climbed into bed and closed her eyes,
grateful Shayne wouldn't remember the events of
the past few hours. The look on his face when he
realized she had betrayed him flashed across her
mind. She never wanted to see that face on him
again.

***

The first rays of the larger sun crept into the
cave and Nolan sat up with a start. He hadn't meant
to fall asleep. Anxious, he picked up his gun and
glanced around. Celeste and Gita were still sleeping,
and the man they had tied up hadn't moved, covered
with the blanket Nolan tucked around him.

Nolan crept over to him. Had he died in the
night? The Dyken's chest moved. Still breathing.

Good. In the daylight he could see a large gash on the side of the man's head still oozing a little blood. His fair skin stood in contrast to the dark, crusty blood on his face. His light red hair was cropped short, and his muscles were well defined beneath his black clothes.

Birds chirped in the trees outside the cave. Gita and Celeste would soon be awake. Nolan stood and stretched his long legs. At least there was room to stand in the first part of this cave. Farther in…that was a different story. This winter would be rough.

Nolan gathered an armful of wood from the pile on the side of the cave. Better get the morning fire ready. He positioned the wood inside the circle of rocks and pointed at it. Flames shot out of his finger and ignited the timber.

Celeste stirred and sat up. "What would you like for breakfast?"

"Bacon and eggs."

"Rice and berries you say? Sure. We have that." Celeste snuck over to her pack. "But first I'm going to the back of the cave to get dressed. No peeking."

"You're no fun."

Two minutes later Gita scrambled out of her sleeping bag, her pink-footed pajamas looking out of place in the cave. "Daddy, I'm cold." She took three steps toward him and stopped. "Who is that?" She rushed over to the Dyken and knelt down.

Celeste stalked over to her. "That's a bad man, honey. Don't touch him."

Gita peered up at her mother, her eyes round. "But mommy, he has an owie."

"He's dangerous." Celeste pulled Gita back. "Don't go near him."

An empty feeling spread through Nolan's chest. Celeste would not allow his daughter to heal him either. She'd rather watch the man die. What has this war done to his wife?

Gita stared at the man while Celeste prepared to cook the rice. "Daddy, is this the man that took Grandma away?"

The question stung him. "I don't know, sweetie."

Celeste pinched her lips into a tight line, but didn't say anything.

The man groaned and tried to move his arms under the blanket. Gita yelped and scooted back. Nolan came over and knelt beside him.

The Dyken's eyelids fluttered open and his gaze traveled to Nolan's face. His thoughts were jumbled, but one thing was clear. He was frightened. "Where am I?" he asked in a raspy voice.

"You're in a cave in the mountains. What is your name?" Nolan heard his wife click her tongue against her teeth in a disapproving manner. He turned to her. "What?"

"We do not need to know his name. We know who he is."

Nolan frowned at his wife and took his attention back to the Dyken. "Your name?"

"Kellec." *I shouldn't have said that.*

"What were you doing in the mountains, Kellec?" Nolan asked, keeping his voice calm.

Kellec struggled against the ropes and winced. "Please, untie me."

Celeste snorted. "No way in–"

"Celeste!" Nolan glared at his wife.

A small portion of guilt flashed across her face before she returned to attending the rice.

Kellec's breathing was shallow. Nolan tried again. "Kellec, tell me what you were doing in the mountains. Were you trying to capture us?"

"Not you." Kellec closed his eyes. *It was a trap. I should have seen it coming.*

"What was a trap?"

Kellec fell back into unconsciousness.

***

Danielle woke early, anxious to see Shayne, to make sure everything was fine between them. Feeling like a robot, she got ready and left for class, not remembering if she had eaten breakfast. After Biology she figured she hadn't because her stomach assaulted her with waves of hunger.

She stopped by the cafeteria to grab a sandwich, and then headed to the testing center. Half the questions didn't make sense to her, but she left not even caring. Now she could stop by and see Shayne.

She swallowed the lump in her throat as she stepped to his door. She pressed the doorbell and stood back, waiting for him to answer.

Shayne opened the door, a look of mild curiosity on his face. The cut on his forehead was gone, probably repaired by Dyken medical officers before he'd been placed back in the Holodome. His eyes traveled over her, a slight smile playing on his lips.

"Hello. What can I do for you?"

She realized she didn't know what memories they had left him with. Did he remember their kiss? Or that they were supposed to go out again? She shifted from one foot to the other, unsure of what to say. "Hi. I just wanted to come by today and see–"

Brady appeared behind Shayne. "Hey, Danielle." He frantically waved his hand across his neck, apparently wanting her to stop talking. "Great to see you. Come on in."

Shayne stepped aside. "Ah, one of your friends."

A sinking feeling started in the pit of her stomach. When she didn't move, Brady ushered her inside and closed the door behind her. "Shayne, this is Danielle. Danielle, this is my roommate Shayne."

He didn't remember her at all. They wiped all of it away. How could they do that? Her stomach clenched tight and she couldn't breathe. He stared at her, his eyes holding no emotion. She forced a smile onto her face.

"Hi Shayne, nice to meet you."

Chapter 6

Shayne gave Danielle a polite nod before turning his attention back to the pile of books on the loveseat. He hadn't felt well this morning, so he'd skipped his classes and now he needed to study.

"Uh, Danielle," Brady said. "Why don't you come with me and I'll get that study guide for you that we talked about." He motioned to her to follow him back into his bedroom.

Shayne rolled his eyes. Obviously she wasn't there to get a study guide. He could practically see Brady making it up in his head. Sighing, he put his feet up on the coffee table. He couldn't care less if Brady wanted to sneak a girl back to his bedroom. It was against the rules, but it's not like he was going to tattle on him.

***

Danielle plopped down on Brady's bed, putting her head in her hands. Her stomach felt like a cold rock in her belly.

"What happened?"

Brady shook his head. "I don't know much. They had some trouble with his resequencing, and had to wipe all memories of you." He pulled out his computer chair and sat backwards, straddling the backrest.

"Good heavens, what am I going to do now? My roommate wants to double date with you and Shayne doesn't even know who I am."

Brady's eyes lit up. "Is she cute?"

Danielle slugged him on the arm. "Focus. What are we going to do?"

Brady shrugged. "It shouldn't be that hard. His memories are gone, but his personality's the same. He thought you were cute yesterday, I'm sure that hasn't changed. Just hang out with him for a while and you'll hit it off again."

Danielle took a deep breath. Brady was right; this could be repaired. "Okay. But there's still the problem with Jennaya. She's expecting a double date tonight. She's going to notice if Shayne is acting like he just met me."

Brady stood, a half-smile on his face. "I've got the perfect solution. Come with me." He grabbed her by the elbow and pulled her into the living room. "Hey, Shayne, Danielle's got a problem I think you can help her out with."

He glanced up from his books, his ice blue eyes meeting hers, and she caught her breath. "Sure. What'cha need?"

"Well, Danielle's been telling her roommate she's got a boyfriend, and now her roommate wants to meet him."

The bottom dropped out of her stomach, and she pinched the back of Brady's arm. Brady didn't react. "So I was thinking you could pretend to be her boyfriend, y'know, just to get her roommate off her back." He grinned, showing all his teeth, like he had just said something brilliant.

The corners of Shayne's mouth twitched, as if he was trying to keep a straight face. "All right," he said tentatively.

Brady rubbed his hands together. "Great. She's thinking we could go on a double date tonight. Are you free?"

"Just a minute," Danielle interrupted. "I need to talk to you," she said tugging on Brady, dragging him to his room. She shut the door and rounded on him. "*That's* your big plan? Making me look like a desperate, lying idiot?"

"Hey, this fixes everything. It gives you an excuse to spend time with him, and now he'll go along with whatever your roommate says."

"Yes. Except now he's thinking I'm a total loser who can't get a date!"

A frown crossed Brady's face. "He won't think that. Come on, let's go talk to him." He went back into the living room, giving her no choice but to follow. Anger and humiliation burned inside of her.

"So, what about it," he said to Shayne. "You doing anything tonight?"

Danielle felt her cheeks grow hot. Shayne interlocked his fingers and put his hands behind his head. He seemed to be enjoying this.

"I don't have any plans."

"Super." Brady turned to her. "You can text Jennaya and tell her it's on for tonight. Have her meet us here. We can get a pizza, and then hit a movie." He checked his watch. "I've gotta get going to class. Why don't you two get to know each other a little bit, and I'll be back in an hour."

He fled the dorm room like his life depended on it. It probably did as she had already decided she was going to kill him.

Shayne smiled, the kindness reaching his eyes. "You didn't know Brady was going to say that, did you?"

She fidgeted. "Not really, no."

He moved his books from beside him to the coffee table. "Have a seat."

She walked to the loveseat, her legs feeling stiff. Not knowing what to say, she kept silent, sitting on the edge of the small couch and staring at the shag carpet.

"Brady's a nice guy. He's just a little forward sometimes. You can gracefully bow out of tonight's performance if you'd like."

She cleared her throat, the humiliation making her feel hot all over again. "Actually, my roommate does think she's meeting my boyfriend tonight. If you're okay with it…"

"I'd be happy to." He snapped his book shut. "What do I need to know to play the part of your boyfriend?"

"Well, we've only been on one official date, so I'm not sure if you're actually my–" she stopped short. She hadn't meant to say it that way. She peered at him to see if he noticed.

He didn't flinch. "Okay, our relationship is fairly new. That's good to know. Where did we go on our date?"

"You cooked dinner for me."

He grinned. "That's perfect. I love to cook. What did I make?"

She shifted uncomfortably. He had said he cooked her one of his specialties. It would seem odd if she were to come up with a dish he was so familiar with. But she couldn't lie since Jennaya knew what they ate. "Chicken Cordon Bleu."

His eyebrows shot up. "Really? That's funny. Sounds just like something I would make." He chuckled. "I guess Brady knows what he's doing. What did we do after dinner? Did we go anywhere?"

That was an easy one. "We watched television for a while, and then you walked me home."

"Where do you live?"

"First and Ash." His intense gaze made her stomach flutter. She shifted on the edge of the seat, trying to put as much distance between them as possible.

"I know where that is. Do we have any classes together?"

"No."

"Okay. How did we meet?"

I was sent to kidnap you. She definitely couldn't say that. "You fell asleep studying on the grass, and I woke you so you wouldn't get a sunburn."

"How very noble of you." He stared at her, obviously formulating what he would say next. "I don't mean to pry, but you seem like a nice girl. You're certainly not lacking in the good-looks department." She felt her cheeks burn once more. "I doubt you'd have trouble getting a date. Why did you lie to your roommate?"

She mulled that over in her head. What could she say that would be believable and yet not pathetic sounding? "Jennaya's always trying to get me to go out with her. I guess I'm not the social butterfly she is. I made up excuses, and she usually left me alone. But last night she wouldn't take no for an answer, saying I needed to meet some guys. So I said I had a date. She got excited and wanted to know all the details. End of story."

He nodded slowly, clasping his hands around his knee. "I see." This seemed to satisfy him. "Is there anything else I should know?" He leaned a little closer, the corners of his mouth curling up in a mischievous grin. "Have I kissed you yet?"

Her bottom chose that moment to slip off the edge of the loveseat, sending her to the floor with a thud. "Oh!" was the first idiotic thing to escape her lips.

Shayne stood and hovered over her, extending his hand. "Are you okay?"

"I'm fine." She took his hand and warmth spread through her. He pulled her to her feet. "Just bruised my ego, that's all."

He smiled, his eyes twinkling. "Is that what they're calling it these days?"

She playfully slugged him on the arm. "You're horrible."

"I'm not that horrible. You can sit next to me without being afraid I'll bite." He motioned to the seat.

"All right. Do you want me to help you study?"

"Sure." He picked up his western civilization book and handed it to her. "We're on chapter seven."

***

Shayne felt Danielle's leg touching his as they sat together on the small loveseat. It was distracting him, making it hard to concentrate on his studies. He closed his book and turned to her. "Do you want something to drink?"

She gazed at him, the freckles on her face giving her a playful look. "Sure. Water is fine."

The Overtaking

He maneuvered his way around the furniture to the kitchen. This girl was unbelievable. Not only was she extremely good looking, but she had a brain and a nice sense of humor as well. Taking a deep breath, he tried to clear his senses. He grabbed two cups from the cupboard, filled them with tap water, and returned to the loveseat.

"Here you go, ma'am." He held out one cup for her.

"Thanks." She took a sip and set it down on the coffee table beside his pile of books.

Sitting down, he tried to ignore her soft floral perfume. "Okay, I think we've gone through the whole chapter. Ask me anything."

She stuck her nose in the book. "Are the social, economic, and political policies in undeviating cohesion with everything that has been facilitated?"

A smile tugged at his lips. "Definitely."

She frowned at him. "Wrong."

"What? I undoubtedly remember undeviating cohesion happening here."

"When?"

"I think it happened when you fell on your ego."

A delightful pink blush touched her cheeks, and she laughed. "Okay, okay, you got me. I'll be serious now."

"Don't change on my account. I like you just how you are."

She looked at him through her eyelashes. "You hardly even know me."

That was true. But he felt like he'd known her for more than two hours. "Good thing we have a date tonight. I can get to know you better."

The front door opened and Brady entered, his backpack slung over one shoulder. "Hey guys, how's it going?"

Danielle's lips tightened into a line, and her eyes narrowed. "Fine," she muttered. She hadn't forgiven Brady yet for throwing her into an uncomfortable situation.

Brady seemed oblivious. "Are you two hitting it off?"

Shayne decided to field that one. "I'd say that the social, economic, and political policies are in undeviating cohesion with everything that has been facilitated." He could see Danielle stifling a smile.

Brady laughed. "Whatever that means. Hey, I'm gonna call in the pizza order. Any preferences?"

Shayne turned toward Danielle.

"I like everything," she said.

He turned back to Brady. "You heard the lady. Get a large and have them put one of everything on it."

Brady groaned. "I should have known better than to ask you. I'm getting a pepperoni." He pulled his phone out of his pocket and started pressing buttons.

Shayne leaned over toward Danielle. "I guess we're eating light tonight. We're all splitting one pepperoni."

Danielle rolled her eyes, but she smiled.

Brady put the phone on his chest. "What time is your roommate coming over?"

"Five-thirty," Danielle said.

Brady put the phone back up to his ear and spoke with the pizza place.

Shayne turned his attention back to Danielle. "Do you know what movie's playing downtown tonight?"

"I think it's that one where the terrorist takes over the train."

Shayne liked the way her nose turned up a little at the end. It was cute. He leaned back, putting his arm over the back of the loveseat. "That one looked good."

She nodded, leaning back also. He couldn't tell if she wanted him to put his arm around her or not. In the end, he decided not to, at least not until her roommate arrived. She hadn't answered him regarding how physical their relationship was supposed to be. The direct approach was probably the best one.

He whispered, "You never answered my question, you know, about whether we've kissed or not."

She whispered back, "I know."

"So?"

Her cheeks turned pink again. "Yes, I told my roommate we kissed. Once. After our date." She didn't look at him.

Her embarrassment made him smile. "Then I would assume it would be appropriate to hold hands during the movie?"

"Only if you want to."

He wasn't sure what that meant. Did she want him to or not? The last thing he wanted to do was make an uncomfortable situation even worse for her. "It's up to you."

If it were up to me, you'd remember.

What was that? The thought just popped into his head. Where did it come from? He didn't even know what it meant. Strange. He decided to ignore it. Danielle smiled up at him. "Then I think it would be very appropriate."

Good. She wanted him to hold her hand. Or, at least, she wanted her roommate to see them holding hands. Hopefully that wasn't the only reason.

Chapter 7

Warm, savory smells filled the cave as Nolan watched Celeste peel the last of their potatoes and cut them into the cast iron pot hanging over the fire. "We'd better find something more to eat in the woods," she said. "Our food is almost gone."

Nolan's stomach growled. "Yes. I'll go search for food tomorrow. There may be some roots we can store and eat."

They could have had all the food they wanted had they not run off to the hills.

Nolan walked over to Kellec. "Awake again, I see."

Kellec stared up at him with light green eyes, silent.

"You're thirsty," Nolan said. "I'll get you some water."

"You can read my mind," Kellec said, "can't you?"

"Yes. Your thoughts are faint, but I can hear them."

Gita looked up from playing in a dirt pile, just outside the cave. "That man hurts."

Nolan brought a canteen over to Kellec. "My name is Nolan. I'm going to lift your head so you can drink."

Kellec nodded. After he had taken a long drink, he lay his head back, and a quiet moan escaped his lips.

"Want to try to sit up?"

The Dyken closed his eyes. "Maybe in a minute."

Nolan studied the man for a while, probing his mind. Kellec didn't seem intent on hurting them. In fact, he got the feeling the man wanted to help them.

"Tell me about your people," Nolan said. "Why are they here?"

"I don't think it's a good idea to talk about that."

Nolan looked around at his meager surroundings. "Why? Are you afraid that if you tell us your top-secret information, we'll go ruin your takeover? Um, I'm sorry to break it to you, but we're just three people living in a cave. And one of us is only six years old. I highly doubt we're any threat."

Kellec's eyes filled with sympathy. "Sorry. I wish I could tell you about what is going on. You might even understand. But it's not in your best interest."

Celeste's head whipped around and she glared at him. "Since when is our best interest any of your concern?"

"I know it doesn't look like it, but your welfare is of great concern to us." Kellec rolled a bit to see Celeste. He gasped and his face wrinkled up in pain.

"I think you have some broken ribs," Nolan said. "Try not to move."

"Yeah. Good idea." He groaned.

Nolan decided to try a different tactic. "My people...they're safe?"

A pause. "Yes, they're all fine."

"Where are they?"

Silence.

Celeste made a scoffing noise. "You don't expect him to answer that, do you?"

"I can try. I get the feeling he wants to tell us."

Kellec's eyes pleaded. "I do want to tell you. But it wouldn't be a good idea."

"All right. Then tell me about yourself. Do you have family? Any brothers or sisters?"

Kellec nodded. "I have two baby sisters who still live at home."

This surprised Nolan. "How old are you?"

"Eighteen."

Nolan raised his eyebrows at his wife. "You're just a kid." Celeste ignored him and fussed with the potato soup.

Kellec didn't respond.

"How old are your sisters?" Nolan asked.

"Fourteen and seventeen."

A light breeze blew smoke from the fire into the cave and Nolan waved it away from his face. "What kinds of things do they like?"

A chuckle came from Kellec. "They like boys. When I was home I would terrorize their dates."

This made Nolan laugh. "A little protective, huh?"

"I suppose so."

Silence fell once again, and an image flashed into Nolan's mind. Two girls stood in the sunlight, one taller than the other, both with light red hair. Kellec's sisters. The sun reflected off a glassy surface behind them. A lake. The taller one pointed to something in the water. When Kellec leaned down she laughed and pushed him in. Kellec smiled at the memory.

"Nolan, would you clean Gita up for dinner?" Celeste asked. She didn't look at him. Nolan knew she had seen it too.

"Sure." He stood. "Time to wash in the stream, Gita."

"Okay, daddy."

He took her hand and led her down the mountain side several yards until they got to the small brook. "Wash your face too. You look like you've been eating dirt."

When he got back to the cave, his wife had dished the soup into the three metal bowls they had. Celeste motioned to Kellec with her chin. "He's hungry. Feed him. I'll eat when he's done."

The Overtaking

***

The doorbell buzzed and Brady stood. Shayne's pulse quickened. It was time to play the part of the boyfriend. Shayne slid his arm around Danielle's shoulder. A smile flashed across her face.

"You must be Jennaya. I'm Brady. Come on in." Brady stepped aside to let Danielle's roommate in. She wore a miniskirt with layered tank tops and two gold hoop earrings dangled from her ears. Brady's grin widened.

"Hi." Jennaya's gaze traveled over Brady. "Nice to meet you." She glanced over at Danielle and wiggled her eyebrows.

"The pizza should be here in a minute," Brady said. "Why don't you have a seat?"

Jennaya walked around the coffee table and sat on the couch catty-corner to the loveseat. "Hi, I'm Jennaya."

Danielle introduced Shayne, and they began to chitchat about school. Brady had just joined Jennaya on the couch when the doorbell rang, making him get up again.

He paid the pizza delivery guy and came back with the box, filling the room with the aroma of cheese and tomato sauce. He opened the lid and set the box on the coffee table. "Dig in."

Everyone grabbed a slice and a silence settled as they ate. Shayne watched Danielle take a dainty bite.

"So," Jennaya said, "did Danielle tell you why we were dripping wet last week?" She stared at Shayne, a half-smile on her face. Confusion swept through Shayne.

No, no, no. Shut up, Jennaya.

It was Danielle, he recognized her voice. Actually, voice was the wrong term. The words hadn't come from her lips. But he was sure the voice had come from her. Before he had time to process this, Danielle shot to her feet.

"Jen, I uh…need to talk to you." She pulled Jennaya into the other room.

Brady frowned. "Girls. Who can understand them?"

Too shocked to speak, Shayne just shrugged. Did he really hear what Danielle was thinking? It couldn't be. Yet he was sure that's exactly what had happened.

He finished chewing the food in his mouth and tried to make sense out of everything. He couldn't. Nothing made sense.

Danielle came back into the room, pulling Jennaya behind her. "Do you like the pizza? I've never had Pizza Barn before."

Jennaya frowned and took her seat next to Brady.

That girl is absolutely out of her mind.

This time Shayne knew the voice was Jennaya's thought. He couldn't explain how he knew; he just did. The surprising thing was it didn't feel odd to him. Something about hearing her thought seemed natural.

The Overtaking

Brady said something to Danielle about the pizza, but Shayne wasn't listening. His mind filled with the thoughts of the people around him. Like a floodgate had opened, voices came at him from every direction. He could hear the people in the dorm room downstairs and the students walking by outside.

He instinctively pulled his mind back and found he could control how much he heard. If he focused, he could listen to one person's thoughts at a time, the rest becoming soft murmurs in the background. A calm, peaceful feeling enveloped him.

It was absurd, but he felt like he had been able to do this all his life. Like a forgotten childhood memory once restored, the voices felt right and complete. The experience made him feel whole, as if he'd only been half a person before.

He realized Danielle was staring at him. *There's something wrong with Shayne. I hope he's not remembering anything.*

Confused, but not wanting to show it, he smiled and looked down at the pizza. "Pizza Barn is my new favorite." He took a generous bite to make his point.

Everyone seemed to relax. Danielle's face smoothed into a slight grin, and she grabbed another slice.

Shayne focused on the thoughts of those around him. Jennaya thought Brady was hot. Brady liked the way Jennaya smiled, but was holding back emotionally. Something about leaving in a few weeks and wouldn't want to get attached. Shane didn't quite know what that meant. Brady had just started his senior year. This college prep boarding school was hard to get into. Surely he wouldn't be thinking of transferring to another school.

Danielle's thoughts were jumbled and much of the time didn't make sense. She was worried about Shayne remembering something, but for the life of him he couldn't understand what she was thinking. Had he met her before and forgotten about the incident? It was possible, he supposed. If she had done something embarrassing, she might not want him to recognize her. He decided not to worry about it. He'd figure her secret out soon, if she didn't stop thinking about it.

A shiver of excitement ran through him. Being able to hear thoughts could come in handy. He could think of all sorts of times it could benefit him, which made him smile.

When they had devoured the food, Brady stood and looked at his watch. "We should head out if we want to catch the show. Do you want to take my car, or should we walk?"

"We can walk. It's only a couple of blocks away," Shayne said.

The girls grabbed their purses and Brady picked up the empty pizza box. He folded it and threw it in the kitchen trash. Then they all followed Shayne outside.

Dusk had set in, but it was still light enough to see. Shayne slipped his arm around Danielle's shoulders.

What a cute couple they make, Jennaya thought.

Danielle was thinking she might hyperventilate. Shayne took that as a good thing and squeezed her shoulder.

After they sat down in the theater, Shayne took Danielle's hand, mostly to see what reaction she would give him.

I can't believe I'm on a sympathy date. Shayne thinks I lied to my roommate. What a pathetic loser he must think I am. And now I can't tell if he's holding my hand because he wants to, or if he's playing the part Brady forced him to play.

Her tortured thoughts continued. Shayne leaned over and whispered, "If you don't mind, I'd like to go on another pretend date with you. This is fun."

She smiled at him, and her thoughts turned fuzzy. "I'd love to."

The lights dimmed and the previews started. While the theater quieted down, Shayne played around with manipulating his newfound powers. He could not only hear people, but he could sense them too. If he extended his mind behind him, he could count those who sat back there. The space around him held energy and when someone occupied a space it interrupted that force.

Danielle squeezed his hand. The movie had started, and the scene had turned bloody. "You okay?" he asked.

She nodded. *This is scarier than I thought it would be. I'm going to have nightmares tonight.*

Victorine E. Lieske

"You want some popcorn?" Shayne asked, holding the bucket out to Danielle.

"Sure." She grabbed a handful and passed the bucket to Brady.

Shayne spent the rest of the movie trying to distract Danielle. Fortunately, it was easy enough. All he had to do was run his fingers over the back of her hand or put his arm around her, and she would stop thinking about the movie.

After they filed out of the theater, Danielle and Brady left to use the restrooms. Jennaya leaned up against the wall and eyeballed Shayne. An uncomfortable silence sat between them.

Shayne cleared his throat. "What was that in the dorm room? When Danielle carted you out of the room?"

Jennaya gave him an eye roll. "Danielle said you don't remember the first time you met and not to mention it because she didn't want to embarrass you. But how stupid is that? So what if you don't remember it was Danielle who woke you up. She should just tell you it was her and be done with it."

Shayne frowned. Danielle had said something about saving him from a sunburn, but that was just a story. Right? "When was this?"

"Last week. Remember, you fell asleep studying on the grass. Danielle and I had been goofing around..." She continued to relate the story, and as she spoke, her memory of that day filled his mind. He saw Danielle reading, and the fight for the book, and both of them ending up in the water fountain. He saw his own body, lying on the grass as the girls approached. Jennaya thought he was cute, but she left that part out of her verbal account. Jennaya pushed Danielle toward him, and he saw Danielle wake him up.

It was strange; seeing himself through someone else's memory felt odd. And he had no recollection of that day. But he knew Jennaya had experienced it, for her memory was so vivid. Confusion edged its way into his mind. What was this all about?

"You really don't remember this at all, do you?" Jennaya asked, her eyebrows knit together. *Maybe he's got Alzheimer's.*

Shayne laughed. "Actually, I do remember now. I just didn't realize it was you and Danielle, that's all," he lied.

"I knew it. I told her to explain it to you, and you'd remember."

"Well, I don't want to upset Danielle, so we'll pretend we didn't have this conversation. It doesn't really matter anyway, does it?"

She folded her arms. "You're right. It doesn't matter. Mum's the word."

***

The cool night air chilled Danielle as they walked home from the theater. Shayne seemed to sense this and put his arm around her shoulder.

"Did you like the movie?" Shayne asked.

"It was okay. I was hoping for suspense, but this was more in the horror category," Danielle said, remembering the blood and cringing.

Jennaya turned around. "I loved it. And with the guy at the end that escaped, you just know they're going to make a sequel."

"I'll let you and Brady go to that one. I think I have plans," Danielle said.

When they arrived at the girls' dorm, they all stood and looked at each other. Danielle was hoping for a goodnight kiss, but it seemed awkward with Brady and Jennaya standing right there.

"So," Shayne broke the silence. "This was fun. We should go out again sometime."

That was non-committal. Danielle's heart sank.

Brady rocked back on his heels. "Yeah, let's do."

Shayne leaned down. "Goodnight," he whispered and gave her a quick peck on her cheek. She wanted to pull him close, but resisted, and Shayne took a step back. Looking at him made her heart race.

"Bye," Jennaya said, starting up the stairs to their dorm room.

They were about to leave, and Danielle felt a twinge of panic. Shayne hadn't asked her out. When would she see him again?

As if on cue, Shayne reached for her hand. "Want to come over tomorrow? We can hang out at my dorm. Maybe I'll make you another home cooked meal." He winked.

Memories of the last meal he made for her popped into her head. She could definitely go for some more of his cooking. "Sure."

A strange look crossed Shayne's face, and Danielle didn't know how to translate it. Before she had the chance to dwell on it the look disappeared and his usual smile appeared. "Great. I'll see you tomorrow. Come over whenever. I'll be around."

By this time Jennaya had disappeared into the dorm and Brady was meandering about. "You ready?" Brady called out.

"Yep." Shayne squeezed her hand and let go. "Bye, Danielle." He joined Brady and the two of them walked off, disappearing around the corner.

***

Conrad Hereth sat at his large oak desk, pushing papers around. The last rays of sunlight had slipped below the horizon an hour ago. Unmotivated to finish grading papers, he stood and walked over to the window.

Living alone had its advantages and disadvantages. In times like these, Conrad wished he had someone to go home to. He stared out of the window, not seeing the campus. Lydia had died ten years ago, and he still couldn't get over her. The familiar hole in his chest deepened.

He ran his hand over his arm, feeling the small bump that had been getting larger each day. Letting his thoughts drift back to reality, he frowned and lifted his sleeve to look at the swelling red welt.

It was dark in the center and almost looked like shrapnel. Strange. He'd never had any kind of incident where he'd get shrapnel in his arm.

Whatever it was, it didn't look like it was going to go away on its own. Lydia would have made him go see a doctor by now. He sighed. He might have to get it checked out.

Chapter 8

Shayne had to take long strides to keep up with Brady, but he barely noticed. He was too concerned about what was going on. Danielle's thoughts were clear. He did cook for her in his dorm room. Her memory of the incident was strong in her mind. The plastic cups, the chicken cordon bleu…she had enjoyed the meal.

But that hadn't happened. It couldn't have. He would have remembered. He stopped, his breath catching in his throat. That's what Danielle had been obsessing about.

Brady turned around. "You okay?"

Shayne nodded and started walking again. "Sorry, there's a rock in my shoe."

Brady shrugged. "Do you want to stop and take it out?"

"No. I'll get it out when we get home."

They continued in silence with the quick pace. Something really strange was going on. And it had everything to do with his memories.

First Jennaya, and now Danielle. They had both remembered him from before today. But he was sure he had never seen either one of them. And Danielle knew this. Not only did she understand and accept he had no recollection of ever meeting her, all night she kept hoping he wouldn't remember her. No, that was not quite right. She hoped he wouldn't remember *again*.

What did that mean?

They reached their dorm and Brady jogged up the steps. "I've got to check my email."

Shayne heard what Brady said, but that was not what he was thinking. He's got to check 'in,' whatever that means.

Brady reached over and nudged his head. "You okay, space case?"

"What?"

"Come on, you've been spacey all night. Heck, you hardly paid any attention to the movie. I'll bet you don't even know the main character's name."

"Darrin."

Brady smirked. "No."

"Derrick?"

"Nope," Brady said. "But you're close. If you keep guessing you'll eventually get it. Unfortunately I don't have the time to wait." He stuck his key in the door and slipped through, obviously in a hurry to get on his computer.

Shayne didn't know what was going on, but had a feeling it wasn't good. Stepping into the dorm, he concentrated on Brady's thoughts. Brady was in his room, with the door shut.

I hope they don't mind I'm a little late logging in tonight, but what do they expect? I'm in the field. They're lucky to get the reports when I have time to slip away. There was a pause in his thoughts.

This time the memory resequencing on Shayne seems to have gone smoothly. There's no sign that his memories are returning, even though he's spent time with Danielle today. He obviously didn't recognize her. I see no sign of his powers returning either. I'll check in tomorrow night as specified.

Shayne's mind reeled. *This time* the memory resequencing had gone smoothly? They changed his memories...and more than once. And Brady knew about his ability to read minds. Something terrible was going on. He walked down the hall to his bedroom and plopped down on his bed. A cold feeling in the pit of his stomach made him want to throw up. Who were these people, and what do they want with him? Was he some kind of government experiment?

He could barely think as he got ready for bed. While he brushed his teeth, Brady entered the bathroom, flashing him a smile. Fear tingled down Shayne's spine. This was all an act. Brady was playing a part, and Shayne was a lab rat.

Realization struck him, and he froze. *Danielle was in on it too.*

***

Kellec slowly became aware of his surroundings. The morning birds chirped, and the woolen blanket on him felt almost rough against his fingers. A scuffling sound came from somewhere in the cave. He opened his eyes and turned his head toward the noise. Pain shot through him. He couldn't help but gasp.

Celeste looked up from the pack she was fiddling with. Tall and slender, she wore designer jeans and a blouse. Not usually what one would wear while camping out in a cave. "You're awake, finally," she said.

"Yes." His voice came out as a croak. Celeste eyed him almost suspiciously.

"Where's Nolan and the little girl?"

"They've gone hunting for food." Celeste pulled a bottle out of her pack and poured some kind of cream onto her hand. She smoothed it over the dark skin of her hands and arms. A coconut smell wafted over to him.

"Lotion?"

Celeste frowned. "My skin gets dry."

"You're not used to camping, are you?"

"No." Her answer came out curt, but Kellec didn't blame her. She didn't know they would be better off if they had let themselves be captured. They'd have a warm home and food to eat. But he couldn't explain it to her. So he kept quiet and tried to think of something else. Would he ever see his family again? Or would he die on the floor of this cave, tied up like a criminal? He supposed to them he was a criminal.

"Are you hungry?" Celeste asked. "We have a few berries."

A few? He wondered how long these people could last out here. "No, thank you." He would wait until Nolan got back with more food; he didn't need to be eating the rest of hers.

Celeste stared at him and he couldn't read her facial expression. "All right." She grabbed a log from the side of the cave and added it to the fire. The flames licked at it.

She sat down, cross-legged, by the fire and warmed her hands. "When I was a little girl, my mother would tell me stories, mostly made up stuff about princesses and castles. They were cheesy, but I loved them. I always said I would record her telling those stories, so I could pass them on to my grandchildren." Celeste turned to face him. "But I never got around to it. And now she's gone."

Sadness for her filled his heart. He couldn't tell her that her mother wasn't gone. She was living, safe and sound, not too far away from here. There was no point in trying to convince her that the takeover was necessary, that they were *saving* their lives, not ruining them. "I'm sorry." Why did he say that? That was totally lame. Pain stabbed at his chest and he exhaled.

Again, the woman stared at him, her face unreadable. "How did you get hurt?"

He struggled for breath. "Some of your people ambushed me. They couldn't see me since I was cloaked, so they swung tree limbs and clubs around until they hit me. And then they kept going. I guess they took their frustrations out on me."

The memory of that day came to him like an unwanted guest. He was in the woods, sent out to get the last High Council member. She was gathering sticks, alone. They always took people when they were alone. His partner waited while he used his paralyze gun and caught her before she hit the ground. Twenty people rushed at him; some hidden under piles of leaves while others dropped down from the trees.

They swung their makeshift weapons until one of them hit him on the side of the head. Pain erupted through his skull. One of them yelled, "Here he is!"

They circled him, pummeling him, and shouting cries of triumph. When a hole opened in their circle, he dove through it and managed to get away, still cloaked. He wandered in the woods for the rest of the day before blacking out. He wasn't sure how he became uncloaked or how he got into the cave. Maybe Nolan found him and dragged him up here.

Celeste frowned. "They were trying to defend themselves."

"I know." The pain made him shake. He stared at the ceiling of the cave. It was just bumpy rock with a few cracks. No stalactites or anything cool like that.

"We have a right to defend ourselves."

His chest felt heavy and cold, like something metal was pressing down on him. "Yes, you do." It was becoming harder to breathe. He closed his eyes. Sleep. That's what he needed.

"Kellec?" It was Celeste. She was calling him, but he didn't want to look at her. He just wanted to sleep.

He felt her hands on his face. "Kellec, look at me." Warmth seemed to radiate from her hands, filling his head. The heat traveled down his body, through his chest, easing his pain, dispelling it. The heat intensified, but didn't feel uncomfortable as it coursed through him. Moments passed, but time seemed suspended, and then the heat drained away as if someone had pulled out a plug.

He could breathe again. He opened his eyes. Celeste's face filled his vision, lines of concern etched in between her brows. "Kellec?"

Energy surged through him and he sat up, the gray blanket falling to his lap. "What did you do to me?"

Her face relaxed. "I healed you."

This information reeled through Kellec. Her power. She could heal. Gratitude overwhelmed him, and then confusion. Why did she heal him? He was the enemy.

"You were dying," she said, answering his thoughts.

He brought his hands to his face, still tied up, and wiped at his eyes. Tears. Now he was going to cry like a baby. Great.

"Thank you," he said, emotion strangling his words.

Celeste looked away and didn't say anything.

***

Danielle fussed around her dorm room, putting the dishes away and straightening up. It was still early, and she didn't want to head over to Shayne's quite yet. He hadn't actually said what time he wanted her to come over, and she didn't want to appear too eager. So she continued to clean her dorm.

Just as she finished scrubbing the bathroom, Jennaya walked in. "You expecting the president or something?"

"No," Danielle said, rolling her eyes. "What's wrong with cleaning?"

"Nothing, it's just that you've been at it for several hours now. I thought you were going over to Shayne's today."

"I am. But I didn't want to go over too early. Is it late enough now?" The butterflies in her stomach woke up.

"Get out of here. If you don't go over there soon, there'll be large holes in the floor where you've scrubbed it clean through."

Danielle stood. "Very funny." She pulled off her yellow rubber gloves and stuck them under the sink with the cleaner and yellow sponge. "As long as you don't think it's too early…"

"Sheesh, girl. He's probably wondering where you are."

The thought made Danielle smile. Maybe he was waiting for her. She ran a brush through her straight brown hair. If only it wasn't so plain looking. Grabbing a hair tie, she pulled it back into a ponytail at the base of her neck. There. That was a little better.

Jennaya curled up on the couch in the living room. "Have fun. Tell Brady I said hi."

"Do you want to come with?"

Jennaya frowned. "No, that's okay. He didn't invite me, and I don't want to be pushy."

"Okay." Danielle reached for the front door. "Bye."

The walk to Shayne's dorm seemed longer than usual, which gave her butterflies time to multiply. By the time she got there, the nerves had taken over. She took a deep breath. What was wrong with her? She pressed the doorbell.

A few moments passed before the door opened. Brady stood in the doorway, a slight smile on his face. "Hey, Danielle."

"Hi, Brady. Is Shayne here?" She wiped her palms on her jeans.

"Yeah, come on in."

Danielle walked to the coffee table and picked up the book on the top of a stack. "Physics? Who's studying physics?"

Brady grinned. "That's mine, although I don't know if you can call it studying. It's more like sleeping through class and making up the answers on the exams."

"Yeah, I don't know how he stays in school." Shayne was leaning against the arch that lead down the hall, his arms folded. She hadn't noticed him there a second ago. He wore a white t-shirt and jeans that fit him nicely. Danielle tried not to swallow her tongue.

"I'm just a good guesser, bro."

Shayne nodded. "Hi, Danielle." His eyes were cool, and Danielle got the vibe he was upset about something.

"Well, I've got to go pick up some things at the grocery store. Do you need anything, Shayne?" Brady asked.

"No, I'm good." Shayne continued to stare at Danielle.

Brady picked up his car keys and left. An awkward silence filled the room, Shayne still leaning against the arch.

Danielle cleared her throat. "What did you want to do today? I wasn't sure what 'hang out' meant."

Shayne seemed to snap out of whatever mood he was in. He walked over to the television and picked up some kind of game console, grinning. "I borrowed this from the guys downstairs. I thought we could have a Super Sports match." The smile fell from his face. "Unless you don't like video games…"

"Sure, I like video games. I'd love a Super whatever match."

Shayne smirked. "Sure you would. You're such a terrible liar."

If only he knew all the things I'm lying about. She swallowed and tried not to think about it. "I've never played that game before, but I'm a fast learner. I really want to try." And she meant it.

"Okay. I'll just get this set up."

***

With the game console hooked up, Shayne handed Danielle a controller and sat beside her on the small loveseat that faced the television. As he watched her, his stomach tightened. She was lying to him; there was no doubt about it. Whatever was going on, she was in on it.

He thought about sending her home; saying he didn't feel good would prove easy. He could suggest he was coming down with the flu. But he needed answers. So he pretended everything was fine.

Danielle turned to him. "What does this button do?"

He explained the different knobs, showing her how to hold the controller. She smiled at him. Shayne's chest felt hollow, knowing she wasn't what she appeared to be.

While they played the video game, Danielle's skill improved quickly. "You're getting good at this," he said.

"Thanks."

"Are you from around here?"

Her mind seemed to tense, as if the question unnerved her. Good. He wanted to rattle her. "No, I'm from Washington State."

"What brings you here?"

She maneuvered her controls, completing her ski jump on the television screen, earning a better score than him. With a satisfied smile on her face, she turned to him. "My dad went to this boarding school."

"Is that the only reason you're here?"

"Pretty much." He wasn't getting anything from her mind, except the video game. Apparently she really wanted to beat him.

"Well, I don't remember why I'm here."

She dropped her controller, her head snapping around to him, her eyes wide. "What?" *Dear heavens, no. Not more memory troubles. Please. I don't know what another resequencing would do to him.*

Now that was interesting. Fear and panic shone in her eyes. Her concern for him seemed convincing, even genuine. Then why would she change his memories in the first place?

"I meant that I'm not sure why I ended up at this boarding school. When my mother died, my aunt looked at a lot of different ones. I don't remember why she settled on this one. I'm sure she had her reasons."

Her face relaxed, and she bent to pick up the game controller. "Well, I'm glad you ended up here." *Thank goodness. I couldn't stand to go through that again.*

He stared at her. She did care. Her thoughts were almost tender toward him. He leaned a little closer to her. "You've got an eyelash on your face."

She wiped her hand across her cheek. "Did I get it?"

"No." He laughed. "Hold still." His thumb brushed against her face, and images rushed into his mind. She was remembering them, standing in front of her dorm, kissing. A flood of strong emotion rushed through her, and he realized she had real feelings for him. Her emotions were strong, and it shocked him. He removed his hand with a jerk.

She didn't seem to notice. "Is it gone?"

"Yes." His heart pounded. Danielle was falling in love with him. And he obviously had feelings for her at some previous time…a time he couldn't remember.

Shayne stood up, tossing his controller on the loveseat. "Are you thirsty?" Without waiting for her to answer, he rushed over to the kitchen. "I think I've got some Coke in the fridge."

"Sure, I'll take one."

His racing heart didn't stop as he rummaged through the fridge. The same questions repeated through his mind. Why had they changed his memories? What had happened that he couldn't remember? And was he in love with Danielle before his memories were altered?

Grabbing two cans of Coke, he shut the fridge and walked the short distance to the sofa. "Here you go."

She took her can and set it down on the coffee table. "Thanks."

"Sure." He looked at her a moment before returning to her side. The questions swirling around in his head made it hard for him to concentrate.

Danielle won the next five games.

Chapter 9

Hereth held up the small, silver capsule. It had worked its way through his arm, up to the surface of his skin. Finally this afternoon it had broken free.

He turned on the lights over the medicine cabinet so he could see it better. A seam wrapped around the middle.

Carefully, he twisted the two ends of the metal, pulling the capsule apart. A thin coil of film spilled out onto the counter. It appeared to be some kind of microfilm. He wondered what information it might contain.

A cold feeling started in his gut and spread though him. He opened the cabinet and pulled out a small cloth and wrapped the film up. He needed to figure out how to examine it closer.

***

Brady walked into the dorm room, his arms full of grocery bags. They were heavy, and he wanted to get them into the kitchen. Danielle and Shayne sat on the loveseat, playing a video game. "Who's winning?" he asked as he passed them.

"Danielle's slaughtering me," Shayne said.

"Ouch, that's gotta hurt your manly pride." He set the groceries on the counter and started putting them away.

"I know," Shayne said, "She's never even played this game before."

Brady glanced at Danielle. She practically beamed, which made him laugh. "Are you sure Shayne's not letting you win?"

That brought a frown to her face. "Why? Because there's no way a *girl* can be better at a video game?"

"Hey, don't get all worked up over it. I was just teasing." He opened the fridge and slid the milk onto the top shelf.

"Good, because I don't wanna have to teach you a lesson."

"Is that a challenge? I'll be happy to take you on while Shayne's cooking dinner," Brady said.

Danielle laughed. "I was going to help in the kitchen, but maybe I can arrange a few games with you."

"Deal." Brady put the last can in the cupboard and turned around. "But I'm not going easy on you, like Shayne."

Danielle stuck her tongue out at him. Brady slid onto the couch across from Danielle. While they played on the game console, Brady studied them.

The way Danielle looked at Shayne made him nervous. She definitely liked the guy. Maybe too much. When he beat her score, she touched his arm. Her eyes lit up every time he looked at her. She laughed at all of his corny jokes. An uneasy feeling swept through Brady.

When Shayne got up to use the bathroom, Brady leaned over to Danielle. "Hey, you know we're not really going to school here, right?"

A frown crossed her face. "Yeah. So?"

There was no easy way to say this. He just had to blurt it out. "You look like you're really into this guy. Danielle, he's *Maslonian*. You're not even from the same planet."

A noise came from the bathroom, like Shayne had dropped something on the tile floor. Brady glanced over at the hallway, but Shayne didn't appear.

Danielle's face turned red. "I know he's Maslonian. Don't you think I know that?"

"Hey, I'm just looking out for you. We're leaving once we've ensured their stability. This is a temporary assignment. I just don't want you to forget that."

Danielle glanced down at the floor. "I know."

***

Shayne tried to steady himself against the bathroom counter. Not from the same planet? These people were aliens? He shook his head. No. That couldn't be. He must have misunderstood. But as he listened to their thoughts, he knew. They were not from this world.

His heart pounded, and he turned on the faucet to splash cold water on his face. This couldn't be happening. What was he going to do? He was Maslonian. He had no idea what that meant. And they had mentioned they were leaving once *the Maslonians* were stable. Apparently he wasn't the only one they had done this to.

Taking the towel from the rack, he dried his face and hands. Now he had to go out there and pretend he didn't know. Pretend that everything was fine. His stomach flipped.

Opening the door, he shuffled into the hall and through the archway. Danielle sat on the couch. Her eyes glued to the floor.

"Hey, Shayne, what are ya making for dinner?" Brady asked.

"Spaghetti."

Danielle brushed a strand of hair from her face and peered up at him. "Sounds delicious. What would you like me to do?" She stood and maneuvered around the coffee table.

"You can brown the hamburger while I make the sauce."

"Okay."

While they worked together in the kitchen, Shayne eyeballed Danielle. She didn't appear to be physically different from him. No pointy ears or webbed fingers. He couldn't tell by looking at her she was from another planet.

As she drained the hamburger, she smiled at him. "What're you thinking? You've been quiet."

Shayne tried to come up with something plausible. "I was just thinking about my family."

The color left her face. *Please let his created memories be intact.* "Oh? What about your family?"

So they had messed with his memories of his family. He wondered why. "Nothing important, really. I miss my mom."

Sadness filled her eyes. "I'm sorry, Shayne." He knew she meant it.

The corners of her mouth turned down, and memories flooded through Shayne. Danielle's memories. She stood in a small room with white walls. He saw himself, unconscious, carried by several people.

A man with black hair turned to face Danielle. "You want to know why Shayne wasn't stationed with his mother as normal protocol. I'll tell you why. His mother died during the takeover. A dreadful accident that couldn't be avoided. But our last resequencing was too drastic, a mistake we will not repeat. Thank you for your help. Now you may return to your duties in the Holodome."

The memory faded. Shayne stepped back from Danielle. Her people had killed his mother. A lump formed in his throat, and he felt sick.

She touched his arm. "You must have really been close."

Shayne nodded. He couldn't speak. The man's words repeated in his mind. *His mother died during the takeover.* The takeover…of what? Could it be that Danielle's race invaded his planet and wiped everyone's memories? His hands shook. Somehow, as they were taking over his people, his mother died.

It looked like Danielle didn't know what else to say. An uncomfortable silence settled between them. Dumping in the hamburger, he mixed it in with the sauce.

Thoughts of his mother swam around in his mind. He wondered how she had died. Had she suffered?

Turning to Danielle, he decided to change the subject. "What about your family? Do they all live in Washington?"

"Yes," she said.

"That must be pretty. They get a lot of rain there, don't they?"

She nodded and pulled a pot from the cupboard. "Do you want me to start boiling the water?"

"Sure."

Danielle was distant during the meal. She poked at her food and didn't talk much. Her thoughts kept going back to what Brady had said to her. Brady, however, rambled on incessantly about whatever popped into his head. Shayne got the feeling he was trying to fill the silence.

After dinner, Brady announced he needed to get some homework done, and he shut himself in his room. Danielle wandered into the living room. "I probably should get going," she said.

His stomach tightened. If she left, he wouldn't be able to glean more information from her. "Are you sure you don't want to stay for a while? It's not even seven o'clock."

Frowning, she twisted her hands together. "I really have to get home." *I need to get out of here. What was I thinking? Brady's right. We're leaving in a few weeks.*

Panic rose in him. She was going to leave and not come back. He said the first thing that came into his mind. "I'll walk you home, then."

Her green eyes met his, and she surrendered. "Okay."

***

Danielle almost sprinted out of the door, eager to get away from Shayne. Unfortunately, he was right behind her. As they walked down the sidewalk, Shayne hooked his thumbs in his pockets. She was glad he didn't try to hold her hand. She didn't think she could handle touching him right now.

"It's a nice evening," he said.

The sun dipped below the horizon, causing streaks of purple and orange to cross the sky. A light breeze blew and the faint smell of barbeque lingered. "It is." The hollow feeling in her chest deepened.

They strolled along in silence, passing a pair of students walking the opposite direction. Maslonians. Most of the students here were Maslonian. Danielle wondered how many Dykens were stationed here. Probably not that many. They really only needed a few to make sure nothing unusual was happening. If anything did happen, the Dykens took care of it. Memory alteration was convenient that way.

They crossed the street to her block. Shayne cleared his throat. "What are you doing tomorrow?"

"I've got to study."

Shayne raised an eyebrow. "Would you like help? I'm a good study partner."

They slowed as they neared her dorm. Some students were tossing a baseball back and forth on the front lawn. She stopped walking and looked up at him. "Shayne, I think we need to talk."

He frowned. "What about?"

"Us. I don't think this is working out." She tried to swallow, but the lump in her throat wouldn't let her.

"I'm not being a very good fake boyfriend. I understand. I can do better." He took her hands in his, but she pulled away.

"I'm serious, Shayne. I can't see you anymore." She turned away to see a baseball headed straight for her face. She didn't have time to duck. The ball was coming at her too fast. Two inches from her nose the ball stopped in mid-air, as if someone had caught it right before it hit her face.

But no one was there. She stared, unbelieving, at the ball suspended in the air.

Shayne reached out and plucked the ball from where it had halted.

"Sorry about that," one of the students yelled. "Nice catch, though."

"Thanks," Shayne called, throwing the ball back.

Alarm flooded through her. Shayne's powers were manifesting. She stared up at him, fear inching its way down her neck. He stared back at her, his eyes wide.

Her gut twisted. She had to go inside and report the incident. He would be taken, and she had no idea what they would do to him this time. It killed her to do it, but she had no choice.

He reached out and touched her shoulders. "Danielle…"

She squirmed away from him. "I have to go."

"Wait…"

Waiting was out of the question. She ran down the sidewalk and up the steps to her dorm room. Only after she opened the door and entered did she realize Shayne was right on her heels. She tried to shut the door, but he stopped it with his foot.

Chapter 10

Kellec leaned against the cave wall, his stomach rumbling. He hadn't allowed Celeste to give him any of the berries, which was good because he could tell she was famished when she finished them for lunch. Now she was cooking the last of the rice. Nolan and Gita hadn't returned, and the concern was growing on her face.

I could go look for them, if she'd untie me. He pushed that thought out of his head. No way would he ask her to do that. She'd never believe him. He'd just look like a bigger jerk than he already appeared to be.

"Did you have mountains near your home back where you're from?" Celeste looked over her shoulder at him.

"Yes, not too far away. Your planet is a lot like my home was before..." He stopped. No. He'd better not talk too much about his home planet. It would be best if she didn't know. She might still be integrated into the Holodome, and he didn't want extra information rattling around in her head for them to have to erase.

Her gaze traveled back to the cast iron pot. "You must miss your home."

"I do."

Crunching sounds came from the woods and Celeste shot to her feet. Nolan and Gita came up the slope, and relief poured over Kellec. Nolan had a large jackrabbit by the hind feet, and Gita carried a basket filled with fruit.

Celeste rushed to her husband, crushing him in a large hug. "I was so worried about you!"

"We're fine. We had an adventure, right, Gita?"

"Yes!"

Nolan stared at Kellec. "You seem to be doing much better." He glanced at his wife, a large grin on his face. Celeste looked at her shoes.

Gita bounced on her toes, her pigtails bobbing up and down. "We saw huge machines taking away the trees," she exclaimed, her eyes lit up.

"What?" Celeste asked. "Machines?"

"They were shiny and they had huge wheels." Gita raised up one of her arms to show how large they were.

Skuttles. Why are they clearing away the trees with them? Confusion ripped through Kellec.

Nolan turned to him. "You know of these things?"

"Yes. They are from my world."

Nolan nodded, and then held up the animal. "We'll talk about this after dinner. I'm going to skin this rabbit."

Gita yelped, and Nolan put his free hand on her shoulder. "Remember what we talked about? We need our strength. It is necessary for us to eat meat."

The little girl nodded, her eyes downcast.

"Now show your mother all of the food we gathered in our packs."

***

Shayne tried not to push too hard on the door. The last thing he wanted to do was hurt Danielle. But he needed to talk with her. "Please, just let me come in."

"Go away."

Her thoughts were frantic, and while he couldn't catch everything she had running through her mind, he did know one thing. She was afraid. "I won't hurt you," he said.

After a pause she stepped back and let go of the door. He nudged it open. Her eyes traveled over his face. "I know," she said, but she tensed as he came in the doorway.

"Really? Because you're acting like you're scared to death of me."

She took another step back. "I know you won't hurt me."

Shayne slid into the dorm room and closed the door. The dim light from the window cast long shadows over the shabby furniture. He flipped on the lamp. "I don't think your roommate is here."

"Jen?" Danielle called without taking her eyes from his face. When there was no answer, she nodded. "You're right. She's not here."

Shayne studied Danielle as she stood, motionless. He had to talk her out of reporting this. His life might depend on it. "Do you want to sit down?" he asked.

She shook her head. "No."

"All right, then we'll talk here." He inched closer to her, trying to find the right words to say. "I know you're scared, but you don't need to be. I would never do anything to harm you."

"I'm not scared of you, Shayne." As soon as the words left her mouth, he knew they were true. Her fear wasn't directed at him. She was afraid *for* him…afraid of what they would do to him after she reported his powers were returning. And she was afraid that if she didn't report it, she would be in terrible trouble.

"Okay, that's good." He was almost close enough to touch her. "Let's just talk about this, okay?"

"I don't think that's a very good idea."

He mulled the situation over in his mind. What did he have to lose? He might as well get everything out in the open. "Because you're afraid your people will have to erase more of my memories if we talk about this, right?"

The color completely drained from her face. "How much do you remember?"

"Nothing. I can't remember anything." He lowered his voice. "But I can hear what everyone around me is thinking."

She swallowed hard. It took her a moment to speak again. "How long...have you been able to?"

"Since last night."

Thoughts of what he might have learned from her ran through her mind. "Tell me what you know."

Shayne closed the distance between them. "I know you don't want to report this."

Pain showed on her face. "Then you also know that I have to." Her eyes pleaded with him.

A wave of compassion for her swelled in him. He could feel her inner conflict. "I know that you care for me and that you don't want anything to happen to me." He touched her hand, but she pulled it back.

"And you probably also know I'm not supposed to care for you."

Slowly, but firmly, he took her hand again. Her pulse jumped against his skin. "Yes. I know that," he said.

The image of them standing in front of her dorm kissing jumped into her mind, and she pushed it out, shaking her head.

Shayne smiled. "I can read your mind, you know."

Her cheeks turned pink, and she looked down at the floor. "I know."

Lifting her chin with his finger, he peered into her eyes. "I wish I could remember. We must've had some nice times together."

"Yes, we did."

The pounding of his heart sounded in his ears. He wondered what it had felt like to kiss her. Her green eyes stared into his, and emotion raced through her. Cupping her face in his hands, he gently pressed his lips to hers. She reacted with an eagerness he hadn't expected, wrapping her arms around his neck and pulling him close. The physical sensation of the kiss combined with her strong emotional response made him pull away and gasp.

Her hands flew to her face, and she turned away from him. "I'm sorry. You have to go."

His feelings for her overwhelmed him. Was he remembering how he had felt about her? He wasn't sure. But he did know one thing. If he left right now, she would report him and he would lose his memory of her again. "I can't go, Danielle. You know that." He raked his hand through his hair.

"Shayne, I have to report the incident. They need to know your powers are returning. I'm so sorry, but it's for your own good." She really believed that.

Confusion hit him. "How is it for my own good?"

"You don't remember how your planet was before the takeover. It was awful. Wars covered the land. Your people were on the verge of extinction from killing each other. My people came to help you."

He closed his eyes. Could this be true? "What did it matter to your people?"

"My world was destroyed centuries ago by war. My people almost wiped themselves out too. Luckily, near the end, they took a look at what had happened to the planet and their people and decided to put down their weapons of war. Unfortunately, the planet was practically destroyed. We had to come up with a plan. We used our technology to build a structure that could house what was left of the population and sustain life."

"What kind of structure?"

She folded her arms across her chest. "We called it a Holodome."

He had heard that name before in her memories. *You may return to your duties in the Holodome.* "Is that what you did on my planet? You built a Holodome?"

She nodded. "We're in the Holodome right now. As you can see, it's just like living on a real planet."

"Is everything around us holographic?"

"Not everything. It's a combination of holographic and molecular reconfiguration."

Shayne turned this information around in his mind, trying to grasp it. His people were at war with each other. Danielle's race saved them from extinction. But at what cost? "Why erase our memories and take away our powers? Instead of saving us, didn't you simply imprison us?"

Danielle gazed up at him, her eyebrows knitting together. "With such hatred for each other, you wouldn't have stopped killing. Some things run too deep. We had to erase those tendencies."

Unease swept through him. "But your race was able to rise above it. Aren't you interfering with things that should be left alone? What about our free will? Don't we have the right to choose our own destiny?"

"But you were choosing death and destruction. Look around you. There is no war here. There is no crime. People are happy."

It was a compelling argument, but fear edged its way into his chest. "But we're not free, Danielle."

She sighed, and took a step back. "You're free to go to school. Free to get a job. Free to marry and have a family. You're free to do anything you want!"

"No, I'm not. You're going to get on your computer and someone is going to take me away to drill into my head. And when they're done, I won't even remember you. I won't have my powers. I won't be free to be who I really am."

"I don't think they use a drill."

He smirked at her. "That makes me feel a lot better."

The front door opened and Jennaya waltzed in. "Oh. Hi, Shayne." She tossed her purse onto the chair. "What's up?"

"Nothing," he said. "What's up with you?"

Geesh, what did I walk into? Did someone die or something? "I'm just coming in to change. I've been invited to the dance club downtown."

Shayne tried to smooth his face into a smile. "Sounds like fun."

Jennaya brushed past them and entered her bedroom. Danielle walked over to the kitchen. "Shayne, do you want something to drink?"

That was a good sign. At least she wasn't kicking him out anymore. "Sure, what'cha got?"

"Coke, orange juice, and water."

"I'll take some OJ."

Danielle smiled. "What a healthy choice."

As Jennaya fussed around the dorm getting ready to go, Danielle and Shayne sat on the couch sipping their juice. When Jennaya came out of the bathroom, she frowned at them. "Is everything okay with you two?"

"Yes," they both answered.

"All right. I'm headed out. Don't wait up for me, Danielle." She grabbed her purse and dashed out.

Shayne put his hands around his knees. "I guess we aren't very good at pretending everything is fine."

"I guess not." She closed her eyes.

"Listen, Danielle, let's put aside the ethical debate for now. So I can read minds…and apparently catch runaway balls. So what? I won't tell anyone. No one else knows but you and me. I'll make sure no one else finds out. You don't have to report it. No one will take me away, and I won't lose my memories."

She studied his face and contemplated his proposal. "If they find out…"

"What would they do to you?"

"I'd have to leave."

He put his hand on her back. "But your life wouldn't be in danger."

Her head snapped up. "No." And then she understood what he meant. "But your life wouldn't be in danger either. We're not here to hurt people."

"Then what happened to my mother?"

She looked like she had been punched in the stomach. "Oh, Shayne, I'm so sorry. I don't know what happened." She put her head in her hands.

"What if something went wrong with their procedure? What if the same thing happens to me?" Shayne could feel her fear and knew he was hitting a nerve. He knew she didn't believe it was safe. A memory flooded into her head, and he could see Brady talking to her. Shayne frowned. "They had some trouble with my resequencing last time, didn't they?"

Tears filled her eyes, and she nodded.

"Danielle, don't you see, you can't let them mess with my head anymore. I could end up a vegetable, or worse."

As she wiped at her eyes, she said, "Okay. I won't report it."

***

Hereth sat on a chair in the lab. Peering into the microscope, he studied the tiny film that had come from the capsule in his arm. What he found sent shivers of fear though him.

After reading through the entire film twice, he pulled it out of the microscope. Walking as fast as he dare, he left the lab and took the stairs to his office. He placed the microscope slides containing the film into the top drawer of his desk and locked it, pocketing the key.

His entire planet had been taken over, and no one even knew. There could be Dyken spies all around him. He pulled out his roster of students, scanning for one name, the only name he recognized from the film.

Shayne Bartlet.

This is who he needed to contact.

***

"Um," Danielle said, "how does this mind reading thing work, exactly? I mean, can you look into my head and see everything I've ever done?" She swallowed, hoping that wasn't the case. She tried not to think about all of the things she'd done that would upset him.

Shayne laughed, stretching back against the loveseat. "No. I can only catch thoughts and memories as you're thinking them. And I don't always hear everything."

Danielle processed this information. *So, can you hear me now?*

"What are you, a cell phone commercial?"

"It's so weird you can do that." It really didn't creep her out, even though it probably should.

"You'd think it would be strange for me, but honestly, it's not," he said. "It just feels natural."

"How far away can it work?"

He scratched his chin. "From what I can tell, pretty far. Miles, if not farther." This startled her. She had no idea his powers were so strong. The look on her face must have been bad, because he quickly added, "But don't worry, it's not like I'd go home and eavesdrop on you or anything."

"Good." She poked him. "You'd better not." The clock on the wall chimed, and she glanced up. "It's getting late."

"Yes. I need to get home." He shifted in the seat and his face turned serious. "But first, I need to know how things are between us. Am I still your fake boyfriend?"

A lump formed in her throat. She was leaving in a few weeks. Like it or not, she shouldn't continue to see him. "Shayne, I–"

"Wait," he said, putting his finger on her lips. "Don't answer that yet. Give yourself time to think. I'll make us a picnic lunch and we can talk about it more tomorrow." He brushed the backs of his fingers across her cheek. "Okay?"

Her face tingled where he touched her. How could she say no to him? "All right."

***

There hadn't been a lot of meat to split amongst the four of them, but with the rabbit, the rice and the fruit they had found, Nolan felt like he had eaten a feast. He took another swig of water from his canteen. "Celeste, that was delicious."

"I'll have to agree with you on that," Kellec said, leaning his head back on the cave wall.

Celeste smiled at them from the fire where she boiled the water to clean the dishes. Gita had fallen asleep while eating.

Nolan's chest tightened, remembering what he saw this afternoon. "Now, tell me about these machines."

Kellec shifted his weight. "They're called skuttles. They take matter and compress it. They're used to clean up. Large piles of garbage are compressed – or shrunk down if you will – and can be stored in a small area."

"We saw them clearing the land. There were three machines taking down trees at an alarming rate."

"Well, I don't know why they would be taking down trees. Unless…" Kellec swallowed. *Unless they plan on taking the trees back to our planet.*

"Why would your people want our trees?" Nolan asked, a horrible feeling creeping over him.

Kellec put his tied hands up to his forehead. "Oh, no." Nolan felt fear once again enter Kellec. "I need to see this. Can you take me there tomorrow?"

Nolan looked over at Celeste. *I will have to untie him.*

She nodded, her face grave. *Take him tomorrow. I'll stay here with Gita.*

"I will show you in the morning."

The Overtaking

Chapter 11

Shayne pulled the package of subway style bread down from the cupboard. It felt good to be doing something mundane, like making sandwiches. With the revelation that his life wasn't what it appeared to be, his thoughts had been heavy the past twenty-four hours. Pushing that aside to get ready for the picnic gave him a refreshing reprieve.

Brady sauntered into the kitchen. "What are you up to?"

"I'm making a picnic lunch."

A smiled crossed Brady's face as he eyeballed the subs. "For you and Danielle?"

"Yep. We're going over to the Waterfall Gardens, and I thought it would be nice to picnic on the grass."

"Are you putting vinegar salad dressing on the sandwiches?"

"It's my secret ingredient. Makes them taste delicious." Shayne didn't have to hear Brady's thoughts to know what he was thinking. "I'll make you one and stick it in the fridge."

"Hey, thanks, bro," he said, pushing his fist into Shayne's shoulder. "You're the best."

After Brady left, Shayne finished making the sandwiches and packed the lunch in a grocery sack. He loaded his car with the food and a blanket to sit on. At the last second he grabbed a radio, thinking a little music might be nice.

When he pulled up to Danielle's dorm, she hopped into his car. "Hi," she said, fiddling with her seatbelt. She'd left her hair down today, a look that framed her heart-shaped face.

Nervousness overcame him, and his mouth went dry. "Hi." He pulled out onto the street, heading for the interstate.

"Where are we going?"

"I thought we could go to the Waterfall Gardens. I've heard they're beautiful in the fall, and there's a grassy area where we can set up our picnic."

"Sounds nice." There was a slight sadness to her voice, and Shayne wondered what that was about. She wasn't thinking about anything except for the scenery outside. It did strike him as kind of odd that she would care so much about the trees. Then it hit him. Of course, she was trying to hide her thoughts from him.

In an effort to fill the silence, he turned on the stereo. Scanning stations, he found soft rock and adjusted the volume. It was only fifteen miles to the gardens, but Shayne had a sneaky suspicion the drive would be a long one.

Danielle brushed her hair back from her face and stared out the window. Her thoughts continued to flit from one unimportant thing to another. After ten minutes of this, Shayne's annoyance got the better of him. "You didn't have to come, you know."

Hurt showed in Danielle's eyes. "I know. I wanted to."

"Well, you're not acting like it." He gripped the steering wheel, trying not to get angry. "If you want me to butt out of your business, just say so."

"That's not it…exactly." She brushed invisible lint from her jeans. "It's complicated."

"Really? That's how you're leaving it? It's complicated? Is there anything about us that isn't complicated?"

Danielle sighed. "You're right. Everything is complicated. But I don't want to talk about us right now. Let's just enjoy our picnic."

An empty feeling started in Shayne's chest. "Okay. We can talk about our relationship later. But I was hoping you'd answer some questions for me."

She sat for a few moments before she said quietly, "What kind of questions?"

Shayne sped up to pass a truck. "Like, how long ago was I placed in this Holodome?"

Danielle squirmed in her seat. "Why do you want to know?"

"Don't you think I have a right to know?"

Shayne felt a wave of sadness pass through her. "You're right. You do." She sucked in a breath and let it out slowly. "You haven't been in the Holodome for long. A little bit more than a month maybe."

A scene flashed into her mind, but she pushed it out before he could comprehend it. All he saw were the two of them in a room together. He wasn't sure what it meant, so he continued on with his questions. "I know this planet as Earth, but it isn't, is it?"

She twisted her hands together. "No. It's a re-creation of Earth."

"What's the name of this planet? The one outside the Holodome?"

"Maslonia."

That sounded familiar. She and Brady had talked about Maslonians yesterday. "I'm Maslonian, then?"

"Yes."

He glanced in her direction. "And you are…?"

"Dyken."

"Why don't we look any different?" A tingle made its way down his spine. "You're not wearing some kind of…Maslonian skin or something, are you?"

She laughed, but it sounded strained. "No. This is the real me. We're both humanoids."

Shayne let that information sink in while new questions formed in his mind. "Why Earth? Why didn't you re-create the planet you're from?"

"We did. We're from Earth…at least, the planet that used to be Earth."

"Earth is your planet? The one destroyed by war?" The hollow feeling in his chest widened. He knew this planet was not real, that he wasn't even from here, and yet he felt like he had lived on Earth his whole life. To know it had been destroyed centuries ago was hard for him to take.

Danielle turned toward him, her eyes sad. "Yes."

Shayne found it hard to speak. He let the scenery speed by as he took in the trees beginning to change with touches of orange and red. This land…it no longer existed. "How bad is it?" he finally asked.

She looked down at her hands. "Very bad."

He sighed. "Show me."

Thoughts of her home world filled her mind. Shayne saw the land, scorched and desolate. No vegetation grew. Large craters where massive destruction hit were visible through a haze that covered everything. The people clutched gas masks to their faces as they walked along the perimeter of a massive domed structure. The Holodome. A fierce wind blew a cloud of dirt and grime over them. An older man, maybe her father, pressed his palm against the side of the structure and a doorway appeared. The memories faded, and Shayne tried not to be overwhelmed by the feelings coming from Danielle.

"That's awful," he said.

She nodded, but didn't say anything.

His throat constricted. "Is it that bad on my planet?"

"No, not everywhere. I've seen photographs of war-torn areas, but the places where I was on the surface looked good."

At first he was relieved, but then unease replaced it. "If you don't mind, would you show me what it looks like?"

"All right." She closed her eyes, and he could see her standing in the street. Houses lined the sides; their yards trimmed neat. A weeping willow swayed in the breeze as she walked toward one of the small homes. A large sun hung low on the horizon as well as a smaller one higher up in the sky. The setting sun cast pink and orange hues across the landscape. It was breathtaking.

He stole another glance at her. "Thank you. That was beautiful."

"Yes. Your world is worth saving."

Something didn't sit right with this situation. Shayne mulled it over in his head before approaching the subject with her. "Danielle, if my world has places like this, why would your people need to build a Holodome? Why couldn't we live in this area on the surface?"

Danielle frowned. "Much of the planet is destroyed. I don't know that there's a large enough place for everyone to live in."

"And yet, you saw no evidence of war on the surface, did you?"

The muscles in her jaw clenched. "What are you saying?"

"I'm just saying the pieces don't fit together. I'm having a hard time swallowing this." He slowed the car, getting ready to take the exit.

"I'm not lying to you. Look in my head all you want. You'll see."

"I know you believe what you're telling me is true. I'm just not sure I believe it."

With an exasperated sigh, she folded her arms across her chest. "Well, I don't know what to tell you. Why else would we go through all of this trouble?"

He pressed on the brake as they came to the stop sign, his heart thumping against his chest. "That's what I would like to know."

***

Trenton sat at his desk scrolling through computer reports. Things were going as planned in the Holodome. No powers were manifesting, and no one remembered who they were. He smiled as the satisfaction washed over him. He'd done it. Even Shayne Bartlet had been taken care of…for now.

The satisfaction turned flat. If Shayne hadn't been assigned to the Council when he had, Trenton wouldn't have known about the strength of his powers. This unsettled Trenton. There could be others who he didn't know about with extraordinary powers. He didn't like the thought of that.

The computer alerted him to a new email and he clicked to open it.

Trenton – This report just came in. Thought you would like to have a look at it.

He opened the report and read it.

Danielle and Shayne are becoming closer than I feel is good for this mission. I am unsure of what to do in this matter. They are at the Waterfall Gardens this afternoon. Please advise. I fear Danielle will become untrustworthy if she allows herself to become too emotionally involved with the subject.

He had been right all along. Fraternizing with the boy had been brainless. Trenton stood, smoothing out his Dyken uniform. He'd better change. He needed to check this out himself.

***

The trees thinned and the ground turned rockier as Kellec hiked down the mountain following Nolan's trail. His muscles screamed at him. Sitting in the cave for a few days had made him weak. And maybe his lack of food over the past few days had something to do with it.

"Celeste told me you wouldn't eat any of the berries yesterday." Nolan's eyes held emotion.

"She needed them more than I did."

"That's not what I heard," Nolan said. "You almost died."

Kellec felt another wave of gratitude for the people who had saved his life. "It wasn't from not eating."

"That's probably true." Nolan stopped short and Kellec almost plowed into him. "There. See?" Nolan pointed. "Past that hill."

Kellec peered over the land. There they were. Skuttles, like he had thought. Large stretches of land lay in their wake, void of all vegetation. They weren't taking just the trees. They were taking all life.

Nolan turned to him, his eyes searching Kellec's face. "Tell me what this means."

His stomach tightened. "It means they've lied to me."

***

Winding his way through the trees, Shayne slowed the car. Two large open gates and a statue of a soldier with a rifle marked the park entrance. As Shayne eased the car down the path, he stole a glance at Danielle. She sat hunched over, almost frowning. He felt bad for suggesting her people had ulterior motives, but he just couldn't swallow the story she had been fed. And now she was questioning it as well.

He pulled the car over into the gravel parking lot and stopped, shutting off the engine. "We're here."

Danielle smiled, the strained look on her face never quite disappearing. "This is beautiful."

"Do you want to take a walk through the gardens before we set up the picnic?"

"Sure." She unbuckled.

The Overtaking

Shayne rushed to get out so he could open her car door, but she had already hopped out. He frowned. "Gentlemen don't open car doors for ladies where you're from?"

"Shh!" she hissed, pushing his chest. "Someone is going to hear you."

"What? I could be talking about Washington," he whispered.

"Oh. I guess you're right." She put her hands in her back pockets, and Shayne caught a glimpse of what she was thinking. She didn't want him to hold her hand.

His chest felt hollow. She was pulling away from him, physically and emotionally. It didn't take a rocket scientist to figure out what she was going to tell him at the end of their date.

He walked beside her up the stone trail to the top of the man-made waterfalls. There were orange and yellow flowers lining the walkway. They worked their way up the path until they overlooked the falls. Water streamed down a bed of rocks, pooling in several places down the falls. The sound of children playing carried over the rushing noise. He placed his arm around her, and she tensed.

"Hey," he said, "Relax. I don't bite."

She didn't say anything, but her demeanor softened and she didn't squirm away from him. They continued down the path, stopping to watch a pair of children leaning over a pool of water staring at the fish.

"They're so cute." She touched his chest.

Emotions ran through her and he wondered why she would have such a strong response to the children. "Do you have any little brothers or sisters?"

"No," she said.

Then he caught what she was thinking. "Aww, you want kids someday."

She grinned. "I'd love to have kids."

Trying to keep things light, Shayne whispered, "So, tell me about the first time we met."

Danielle stopped, and her thoughts were immediately guarded. "Why?"

That was not the reaction Shayne had anticipated. "Just curious."

"Jennaya and I found you on the grass, asleep. I woke you up," she said, "remember?"

She was obviously keeping something from him, but he didn't want to push it, so he let it go. "Oh, yeah. I remember you saying something about that."

After they walked through the gardens, they went back to the car to get the picnic. Shayne took the keys from his pocket and opened the trunk. As he lifted the radio, he noticed Danielle's face.

Her eyes wide, she tugged on Shayne's arm. "Think about the gardens. Now."

"What?"

"The waterfall. Wasn't it beautiful?" She took the radio from him and shoved it back into the car. "And those kids. They were so cute." She slammed the trunk closed.

The Overtaking

Fear edged its way down his back. Something was wrong. He filled his mind with thoughts of the gardens.

"Get in the car and drive," she said.

Chapter 12

Danielle's pulse pounded in her ears while she tried not to let Shayne see her hands shake. They hopped into the car and Shayne backed out of the parking lot. Danielle forced herself to think about the flowers and the children at the waterfall.

When they were on the highway, Danielle turned around and surveyed the road behind them. No cars were in sight. Trenton hadn't followed them. She sighed with relief. "Our thoughts are safe now."

"Are you sure?" Shayne asked, clenching the steering wheel so tight his knuckles turned white.

"It's okay. We're not being followed."

"But I can still hear the thoughts of people at the park," Shayne said.

"Um, I guess I should tell you. Your powers are stronger than most Maslonians."

His eyebrow lifted. "Really?"

"Yeah. Most Maslonians' telepathic powers don't extend far. Maybe a two block radius. You're...unique."

A look came across his face and he pursed his lips, narrowing his eyes. Danielle wasn't sure what was running through his mind, and he didn't offer up anything to her.

After a moment of waiting, Danielle decided to ask. "What are you thinking?"

"I'm trying to see if I can hear the Maslonian at the park. I'm not finding anyone thinking anything abnormal, but I'm kind of new at this. I could be missing him, or he could have left already. Tell me about him."

Danielle thought of Trenton. When she saw him at the park, he stood by a small sedan. His face was hard and his eyes narrowed into thin slits staring at them. She knew he read Shayne's mind. "His name is Trenton Madison."

"The man with the black hair. I can see him. In fact, I've seen him before in your memories."

"Yes, he is the Maslonian in charge of the special forces. There's only one reason why he'd be here in the Holodome. He suspects you."

"How? I haven't done anything." Shayne eyed her up and down. "You didn't–"

"No. Of course not." She felt hurt that he would even suggest it. "I said I wouldn't. I keep my word."

"Okay. Then who?"

She racked her brain for a minute. "It had to have been Brady. He must have picked up on something."

Shayne shook his head. "Not while I was around. His main concern right now is that you're getting too attached to me."

Brady had told her that too. She realized Brady must have mentioned this in his report. Fear clenched her stomach. "Trenton wasn't there to read your mind," she said. "He was after me."

"What do we do now?"

"I don't know."

"Well, we can't go home. I'm sure he knows where we live."

"What? Of course we have to go home. It will be obvious that something is wrong if we run off somewhere." She took a deep breath trying to calm down. "We have to go home and pretend nothing is wrong."

"That will work really well," he said sarcastically. "We didn't even stay at the park long enough to eat our picnic." He flipped the turn signal on and changed lanes, a frown on his face.

Danielle closed her eyes, knowing what she needed to do. Before she could speak, Shayne turned to her. "No. Don't even think it."

"It's the only way." She peered out of the window at the trees flashing by. "We can't see each other anymore."

He shook his head. "I need you, Danielle."

His words stabbed into her heart, but she pushed the pain away. "I'm sorry. This can't work out anyway. You know that."

"Why? Because I'm not the same race as you?"

"This has nothing to do with race. I'm leaving soon, remember? This won't be long-term no matter what. We might as well stop seeing each other now."

A sigh escaped his lips. "I was hoping you would change your mind about leaving."

"I can't. There's nothing I can do about it."

"Your people wouldn't let you remain here, even if you wanted to? Don't you see that as odd? What is this whole thing really about?"

An uncomfortable feeling made her squirm. "Let's not start this, okay?" He just didn't understand and she couldn't convince him no matter what she said.

He took a breath and let it out slowly. "Fine."

They drove in silence the rest of the way home. When he pulled up in front of her dorm, she turned to him. "I'm sorry. I wish things had gone differently today. I really wanted one last nice time with you before…"

A sad look settled on his face. "I kind of figured you were about to break up with me." He reached out and placed his hand on hers. "Are you sure this is what you want?"

Her breath caught in her throat. "I'm sure."

"Then I guess this is goodbye."

She gathered all of her courage up. "Goodbye." She pulled her hand away from his and opened her car door. Why did she feel like she was going to cry? This was necessary. It wasn't fair to him to keep seeing him, especially after Trenton's radar was set on them. He could be discovered. If she could stay away from him for a little while longer, he would be safe once they left.

She gave him a pathetic sort-of-wave with her hand and started up the walkway to her dorm room. Maybe Jennaya wouldn't be home so she could wallow in solitude. When she got inside, she leaned up against the door and exhaled. This day couldn't get any worse.

Walking toward her room, she figured she should log in. At least if she reported the break up, Trenton might back off. She entered her bedroom and two men grabbed her arms. They were dressed in black. Dyken soldiers.

"What are you doing?" she asked.

"You need to come with us," the tall one said.

"Okay, okay, enough with the hands." She shrugged out of their grasp. "What's going on?"

"Trenton wants to speak with you."

She tried not to let fear take over. "All right."

One of the men opened a portal and they all stepped through. Danielle followed the soldiers down the corridor to a room much like the one they had been in earlier that week. Trenton stood by a table, wearing the same civilian clothing she had seen him wearing at the park. His eyes bored into her.

She stared back at him, allowing her mind to fill with his face, pushing out everything else. "Trenton." The icy way it came out wasn't on purpose, but she didn't mind.

"Ms. Darmok," he said, not trying to hide his displeasure with her. He motioned to a chair. "Please, sit down."

She walked over to the other side of the table and sat. The seat was hard and cold. Trenton continued to stand, making her feel small. "How are things going with Shayne?" he asked.

"I broke up with him," she said flatly.

Trenton narrowed his eyes and folded his arms across his chest. "Really?"

"Yes." The last minutes she spent with Shayne flitted into her head. Shayne's words echoed in her memory. *I kind of figured you were about to break up with me.* Staring at Trenton, she set her jaw. "I told him we can't see each other anymore. I didn't want anything to get in the way of this mission."

"Good. Because I would hate for anything to happen to Mr. Bartlet because of your carelessness, Ms. Darmok."

Danielle shot out of her chair and leaned on the table, her palms flat on the surface, getting as close to his face as she could. "Are you threatening me, Trenton?"

"Not at all, young lady." He stuck his nose in the air. "I'm simply issuing a warning. Now return to the Holodome and leave well enough alone."

Anger boiled deep inside of her. How could he be so arrogant? She shoved herself away from the table and turned toward the door.

"Oh," Trenton said, making her stop in her tracks. "One more thing. If I find out you're seeing Mr. Bartlet again, I'll have no other choice but to take action."

She spun around. "Don't worry. I won't be seeing him again."

He nodded, dismissing her. She dug her fingernails into her palms so he wouldn't see her hands shake. After she left the room, she allowed her anger to wash over her. What a jerk Trenton was. He didn't have to threaten her. She was doing everything she was supposed to do. Well, almost.

She used the portal to take her back to her room. Jennaya still wasn't home. Lying down on her bed, she curled up into a ball. She didn't want to think about what Trenton might have meant by 'take action.'

***

Leaves crunched under Nolan's hiking boots as he led the way back to the cave. Kellec was beginning to trust him, he could feel it. If he didn't get the answers he needed now, he feared he'd never get them. Kellec was planning on convincing him to let him leave, and he didn't want to hold him hostage any longer.

Nolan cleared his throat. "What's really going on here? And don't give me any nonsense about keeping these things from me is for my own good. I deserve to know the truth, especially if I'm going to let you go off on your own."

Kellec trailed after him up the steep hill, grabbing onto a tree trunk for stability. "You're right. You deserve to know the truth." Kellec sighed and rubbed the back of his neck, stepping over a tree root. "Explorers from our planet came back from an excursion and told of a world they had found. A world about to be destroyed by war."

Nolan blinked. "Our world? At war? We haven't had any wars until your people came."

"I'm beginning to see that. But at the time, I believed my leaders. We had no military, so they recruited a large number of young people to come and free your race."

"Wait, free us?" Something didn't feel right. "By kidnapping us?"

"We were told that your race would destroy each other if we didn't change your memories and place you in a non-violent environment."

The uneasy feeling grew in Nolan's gut, but he didn't say anything.

"I see now that this was all a lie. Your planet isn't in danger of destruction…at least not from civil war. I believe my leaders are trying to rebuild my own planet, using your resources."

Nolan let this information sink in. A light breeze blew across his skin, cooling his exertion from the hike. "Where are my people?"

"They're inside a Holodome, a whole world that fits inside one domed structure. They're fine. They don't know they've been taken. They think they're living on a planet called Earth, before technology and small-minded people ruined it."

A strong image came into Nolan's mind of the world Kellec had come from. "Earth? I thought you were from a planet called Dyken."

"My people changed the name after the Great War. There no longer was any Earth left. Some of the people vacated the planet to find a new place to call home. Those that stayed built a structure in which everyone could live. That is where I grew up, in a Holodome, like the one we built here."

"Now they're transporting our trees and vegetation to your planet. But why? Why not just take over this one?"

The corners of Kellec's mouth turned down. "I suspect the majority of my people wouldn't allow that."

Nolan stopped. "But they'll allow this?"

"They don't know about this. Not yet. I have to find my people, the ones that don't know, and tell them. This is why you have to let me go. I have to fix what has been done here."

Nolan knew he spoke the truth, he felt Kellec's emotions surge. "Then I am coming with you."

Kellec's face drained of color. "No. I don't think it's safe."

"I can help. With my mind reading powers and pyrokinetic abilities, together we could have an advantage."

A bird fluttered and took off above the trees. Nolan watched Kellec and heard his indecisive thoughts. "Please, let me come with you."

"All right. But you tell Celeste, not me."

Nolan laughed and slapped Kellec on the back. "Deal."

***

The morning sun streamed through the window as the alarm clock beeped. Shayne concentrated and shut the alarm off mentally, mostly to see if he could. Satisfaction made him smile. He'd been practicing and thought he was getting pretty good at his powers.

While he got ready for his morning classes, he tried not to think about Danielle. He wasn't very successful. An empty feeling enveloped his chest. He'd have to come up with something to take his mind off her.

When he walked into his western civilization class, his teacher stopped him. "I need to speak with you after class."

"Okay." Curious to what Hereth wanted, he probed his teacher's mind as he walked to his seat.

This kid's going to think I'm crazy.

Strange. Shayne sat down in his chair. The time crawled while the class dragged on. The teacher had no more abnormal thoughts while he presented the lecture. Shayne tapped his foot in order to stay awake. He couldn't wait for the class to end.

Finally, when it was time to leave, Hereth nodded to Shayne while gathering his materials. Shayne bustled to the front of the room and stopped beside the teacher.

"What is it you need, Mr. Hereth?"

"Not here. Let's go to my office." He walked out and Shayne hurried to catch up. As they proceeded down the hallway, Shayne caught a bit of nervousness from Hereth. Whatever this was about, Hereth wasn't sure this conversation would go well.

When they entered the small office, he motioned for Shayne to sit. Hereth sat at the large leather chair behind the desk. He took a long look at Shayne before speaking, his mind trying to decide how to start. Something about an important thing Shayne needed to know.

Hereth cleared his throat. "Something happened to me the other day, and I want to tell you about it."

"All right." Shayne wondered if this had anything to do with class.

"I found a piece of metal imbedded in my arm. It was a small capsule that contained information."

A wave of images came into Shayne's mind, the capsule, a roll of tiny film and people being kidnapped. His heart thumped and excitement ran through him.

"You know about the Dykens, don't you?"

The Overtaking

Chapter 13

Hereth couldn't believe what Shayne had said, but before he could speak, Shayne jumped up from his chair and began rambling. "I thought I was the only one. Have your powers surfaced? Can you read minds too? What did the microfilm say exactly? Tell me everything."

"Hold on. You have your powers?"

"Yes." Shayne sat back down on the chair. "I can hear thoughts and move objects with my mind."

The relief that came to Hereth was almost overwhelming. "Good. That means whatever they did to us isn't permanent."

Shayne gripped the armrests. "Who planted that film in your arm?"

"From what I can tell, I did. We were being taken over, our people kidnapped and no one could reach them. We found evidence of memory alteration, so I must have compiled the information onto the film in hopes it would be discovered at a later time."

"What does it say?" Shayne leaned forward, a look of concern on his face.

"It tells the story of our people," Hereth explained. "When the Dykens came to our planet, they professed to be explorers. They wanted to learn about our culture. After spending time with us, they left and we didn't hear back from them. We didn't think much of it until our people started disappearing. The Dykens had come back."

"What did they want with us?"

Hereth sighed. "We think they wanted us out of the way so they could take over the planet."

Shayne frowned at this and squirmed a little in his chair. "How bad was the war on our planet?"

Hereth folded his hands on his desk and sighed. "Unfortunately, it was bad. We didn't have any protection against the Dykens. They had cloaking devices that prevented us from discovering them. I assume they eventually captured all of us and erased our memories."

"No, not the war with the Dykens. The civil war."

"The film didn't mention anything about a civil war."

Shayne stood up again. "That's what I was afraid of. Can I read this film?"

Hereth nodded, getting up from his chair. "Yes, I'll take you to the lab."

As they walked, Shayne stuffed his hands in his pockets. "How did you know I knew about the Dykens?"

"I didn't. The film contains the names of the Council Members. Your name was the only one I recognized."

***

Shayne felt like he was walking through a horror movie, a subdued sense of danger lurking ahead. As he walked closer to Danielle's dorm, he started having second thoughts. She wouldn't be happy to see him or like what he had to say. However, this was necessary. And she needed to face reality.

He trudged up the steps to her door and rapped on it with two knuckles. A moment later Jennaya opened the door and grinned at him. "Hi, Shayne."

"Hey there, Jennaya. Is Danielle home?"

"Nope. She's not home." She winked and jerked her head to the left. "She's in class."

"I know she's in there. Let me in," he said with what he thought sounded like an authoritative voice.

"Sheesh, okay. Don't break the door down or anything." Jennaya stepped back, flinging the door open.

Danielle appeared behind Jennaya and rolled her eyes. "Thanks a lot, Jen."

"Hey, whatever. I tried. You two obviously need to talk, so I'll leave you alone." She stomped off and shut herself up in her bedroom.

Danielle blocked the doorway. "You need to leave. Now." She squared her shoulders.

He played the biggest card in his deck. "Another Maslonian knows about the Dyken takeover."

Her eyes grew big and she grabbed his sleeve, tugging him inside. After she shut the door, she rounded on him. "What? How?"

"Hereth planted an information capsule into his arm before he was kidnapped."

She rubbed her temples. "This can't get any worse."

"Just listen, Danielle. The information in that capsule proves you've been lied to. There was no war on our planet. We weren't killing each other, and we certainly weren't about to destroy the planet. Think about it. You saw no evidence of war on the surface." He took a step forward and she backed up against the door.

"But I was in a remote area that hadn't been–"

"No. That was a lie." He placed his hands on the door on either side of her. "Look at me. Do I look like someone who is capable of being filled with hate? Do any of these people seem like they were once bent on killing each other?"

Her brilliant green eyes stared into his. "But the resequencing…"

"The resequencing changed our memories, Danielle. Not our personalities. Doesn't it make more sense that way?"

Danielle's mind churned as she processed the information. Shayne could tell she was about to concede, so he pressed on. "When you were on the surface of my planet, what kinds of things did you see? Were the people carrying weapons? Anything at all that would indicate this deep seeded hatred for each other?" He brushed his fingers across her cheek. "Can you see me murdering anyone?"

She blinked and shook her head. "No." She touched his chest, spreading hot fire through him.

"You have to help us, Danielle. Your people...what they're doing is wrong." He put his hand on hers. "We have to stop them."

She looked at the floor, her shoulders sagging. "I don't know how."

"You have to get me out of this Holodome."

***

Danielle's pulse quickened and she sucked in a breath. "What? I can't do that."

Shayne tapped her ring. "Of course, you can."

Panic shot through her. This was bad. "No. There're people all over the place. It's too dangerous."

He reached into his pocket and pulled something out, the corners of his mouth curling up causing her breath to catch. "Not if I use this."

When he opened his hand, she saw the cloaking device.

"Where did you get that?" She tried to grab it, but he snatched it away.

"Brady was thinking about using it to spy on us."

"And what happens when Brady realizes it's gone? Shayne, you have to put it back right now."

His face turned serious, and he stared into her eyes. "I have to go out, Danielle. I have to see what is going on. Please say you'll help me."

Guilt spread through her. What was she to do? If she opened a portal for Shayne and he was discovered, things would get very bad. Not only would they resequence him, but she would get into trouble. Terrible trouble. She wasn't sure what they would do to her. She couldn't say yes, not even to those pleading blue eyes. "I'm sorry. I can't."

He nodded, a slight frown on his face. "Okay. I understand." He took her hands in his. "I had to try."

The feel of his skin made her hands tingle, and she found it hard to concentrate. "Tell me you'll put the cloaking device back."

"I'll put it back," he said, rubbing the backs of her hands with his thumbs. He leaned closer. "I've missed you."

Those words made her throat constrict. Or it could have been the feel of his breath on her cheek. "It's only been one day."

"Really? It felt like a lot longer to me." He laced his fingers through hers. "Almost like eternity."

She tried not to wobble as her knees went weak. He leaned down and kissed her, his warm, soft lips sending sparks of energy through her. She pulled her hands out of his grasp and entwined them in his hair, pulling him closer, drinking him in. His strong arms wrapped around her, and she never wanted him to let go.

A surge of emotion swelled within her, and Shayne pulled away. "Dang, girl, you sure know how to make a kiss memorable."

Her cheeks burned, and she turned away. "Sorry."

He took her chin, gently returning her gaze to him. "Don't apologize."

Jennaya's door opening sounded from the hallway. Danielle took a step back from Shayne before Jennaya entered the room. "You two work everything out?"

Danielle's heart dropped down into her shoes. She still couldn't see Shayne. He had to leave and not come back. He'd be in so much danger if they found out he'd been to her dorm room today. She had to get rid of him. "Actually," she said, "I was just telling Shayne we can't see each other anymore."

Shayne raised his eyebrows. "Really? That's what that was?"

Jennaya smirked and rolled her eyes. "Sure, okay. I have to leave. You two do whatever you want. Just don't put me in the middle anymore." She slung a backpack over her shoulder and pushed past them. "See ya."

"Bye," Shayne said, shutting the door after her. "Is she always like this?"

"Sometimes worse."

He smiled, but his eyes held no mirth. "I know what you're going to say, so you don't even have to. I'll leave you alone."

She stared down at the floor. "I'm sorry. I wish things were different."

"I know you do." Shayne grasped the doorknob. "So do I." Before she knew it, he had slipped out. An invisible knife stabbed at her gut. Why had she allowed him to kiss her like that? Now the pain had doubled.

Danielle ran a hand through her hair. Something felt wrong. A sick feeling engulfed her. She looked down at her hand. Her ring was gone.

***

Shayne dashed around the corner, sure that Danielle would be opening her door at any moment. He didn't wait to see. Picking up the pace, he ran across the street and through campus. By the time he got to Hereth's building, he was out of breath. He slowed, taking the steps to the second floor.

Hereth looked up from his paperwork when Shayne entered. "Were you successful?"

"Yes. I got the cloaking device from Brady and the key to the portal from Danielle." He leaned on the wall, trying to catch his breath.

"Did Danielle agree to help you?"

"No. I…distracted her…and slipped the ring from her finger. She already knows I took it." He stopped and listened for Danielle's thoughts. "And she's really mad." He cringed. "I've never heard words like that coming from her."

"We'll deal with her later. I assume Brady doesn't know you have his cloaking device?"

"Right. He had it locked in a safe. I'll be in trouble if he goes to get something and notices it's gone, though, so I'd better hurry." The thought of walking through the portal to the unknown caused his chest to constrict, but he had no choice. Who knew what was going on while they were blissfully living a lie here in the Holodome.

"Do you know how to activate the portal?" Hereth asked.

"Yes, the ring has an outer shaft and an inner metal ring. Twisting them causes the portal to open." He took it out of his pocket and slid it onto his pinky finger. It was still warm from being on Danielle's hand. He swallowed the guilt. There was no time for that. He clipped the cloaking device to his jeans and pressed the button. A slight tingling feeling enveloped him. "Did it work?"

"Amazing." Hereth stood and walked over to him. "I can't see you at all." He reached out and touched his chest. "Just don't run into anyone."

"Yeah, right." A thought came to Shayne. "And I have to stay away from Trenton. He can detect my thoughts."

Hereth frowned. "That traitor. I can't believe he helped the Dykens."

Shayne didn't know what to say, so he just nodded. Then he felt foolish because Hereth couldn't see him.

"How will you get back?"

"I don't know. I'm assuming I can re-open the portal with the ring." At least he hoped that is the way it worked. A tinge of fear crept down his spine.

"All right. You'd better hurry."

Shayne twisted the ring and a rectangle of light appeared in the room. "I'll contact you as soon as I'm back." He took a breath and stepped forward.

Chapter 14

The breath squeezed out of Shayne's lungs, and for a split second he felt like his molecules were vibrating. Then he was through and found himself standing in a brightly lit hallway. The portal door behind him shimmered, making a quiet humming noise, and he could see Hereth standing on the other side staring through to him. A red button on the side of the door glowed. He pressed it and the portal went black. There was a keypad and a raised rectangle made out of glass on the other side of the portal. Shayne wondered what that was for, but he didn't want to contemplate it. Time was short.

He took a minute to feel out his surroundings. Concentrating, he reached his mind through the compound, searching out the people and feeling the layout. The building was not overly populated, and he felt relief. At least he could probably walk around without bumping into a crowd of people.

The hallway had a slight curve to it, extending in a huge circle. There were different sized rooms off the main hallway around the entire dome. He turned to the right and started down the hall.

Two men dressed in black passed by him, not even pausing. The cloaking device must be working fine. He continued, looking for a way out of the dome.

A Dyken approached him from behind, moving at a quick pace. He took a step to avoid him. The man stopped, facing the blank wall. He placed his hand on a small metal plate. The wall disappeared, and he went through into one of the rooms.

After Shayne had walked for a while, he came to more portal doors on his right. One of them glowed, and Shayne backed up. A woman came through, turned, and pressed the red button. The portal closed. She then put her palm up against the glass rectangle under the keypad. A thin green light traveled over the palm of her hand, and a display above the keypad lit up.

Words scrolled across the screen. *Dyken 2831 type in your coordinates.*

This wasn't a good sign. The woman typed in something and the portal lit up, a translucent picture of a bedroom showing beyond the shimmering wall. A light above the portal blinked red for a few seconds, and then turned green. The woman walked through and the portal went black.

So, the way back into the Holodome required a palm scan. Crud. He was stuck here. Shayne shook the thought out of his head. He didn't have time to worry about that now. He'd manage somehow. First he needed to find a way to get outside.

He continued to walk, feeling his way past the walls with his mind. Eventually he came to a large hallway leading to a plain white wall. Empty space lay beyond it. This was it, he could tell. He felt for any Dykens on the other side of the door. Nothing. He placed his palm against the metal plate and it warmed slightly at his touch.

The wall shimmered and vanished, and Shayne slipped through. The bright sunlight from two suns caused him to blink before taking in the scene. He gasped. Large craters scattered across the barren landscape. No vegetation was in sight. A light breeze blew dust into his face.

His planet was desolate.

***

Kellec walked beside Nolan down the deserted street, a stray piece of paper blowing in the wind, skidding along the curb. A few cars were stopped in the middle of the street, parked haphazardly, the rest were sitting in driveways. Not a soul was in sight. The scene was a little unnerving to Kellec, knowing what he did now. Nolan peered around nervously, clutching the strap on his pack.

"Are you sure all of your people are gone?"

"Yes. Most of them left the planet before I was sent into the hills. The rest of them are stationed inside the Holodome, keeping an eye on how things are going."

"That's good. I wouldn't want to be ambushed."

The windows of the deserted homes seem to stare accusingly at Kellec. "Listen, I'm sorry for everything."

Nolan's eyes held compassion. "I know."

They walked along in silence for a few minutes before Nolan spoke again. "You know you're going to have to tell me again what all of your little gadgets do before we get there, right? I don't want to grab the wrong one and put myself to sleep when I meant to turn invisible."

Kellec laughed. "We'll go over it again. We've got another day's journey. I'll make sure you're prepared."

"Are you sure you want to go in and announce yourself?"

"I only have one cloaking device. It makes the most sense for you to use it while I get my orders. You can follow me though the portal into the Holodome. Once inside we can do far more than out here."

Nolan nodded. "Do you think anyone will believe us?"

Kellec searched the horizon, focusing on the cloud of dust blowing from where the skuttles cleared the land. "They'll have to."

***

Danielle pounded on Shayne's dorm room door. Blast him, the insufferable idiot. He was going to get himself resequenced again. "Shayne, open up!"

The door opened, and Brady stepped back, his mouth slightly open. "Danielle? What the heck's going on?"

Danielle shifted from one foot to the other, unsure of what to say. Brady stared at her, obviously expecting an answer. She took a breath. "Sorry, but I need to talk to Shayne. Is he here?"

"No. He left for class this morning and hasn't been back. Come in." Brady ushered her inside. "What's wrong?"

"Nothing." Even she didn't believe her lie. Brady looked at her like she had flowers growing out of her ears. Her head began to spin. "He really isn't here?"

The corners of Brady's mouth turned down. "He's not here, and you shouldn't be either. I have to report you if I see you with him, you know."

Fear gripped her chest. "Please don't report me." She clutched Brady's arm. "I'm sorry, you're right. I shouldn't have come. Just forget I was here."

Brady stared at her, his gaze intense. "Danielle, tell me what's going on."

Danielle closed her eyes. She was in trouble now. Brady would report this and she'd be hauled back in to see Trenton. They might even send her back home. Tears threatened to spill down her cheeks, and she began pacing the floor. "I can't tell you."

Brady folded his thick arms across his chest. "Why not?"

Emotion built up inside her. "Because you'll report me, and they'll send me back home. There's no way they'll let me stay here after what's happened."

"Hey," Brady said, stopping her pacing by grabbing her arms. "I won't report this, okay? Settle down. Tell me what happened, and I'll help you."

She searched Brady's face. Was he telling her the truth? Could she really trust him not to report anything she would say to him? "I don't know, Brady. This is a huge risk you're asking me to take."

He squared his jaw. "Listen, we're here to help these people. If we have to bend the rules a little to do that, then so be it. The goal is to save lives, not to make sure Trenton has a power trip."

She wished she could believe him. That would make this so much easier to have Brady on her side. But something held her back. "I'm sorry. I have to leave. I shouldn't have come. Please don't say anything about this in your report. I promise not to bother Shayne any more." She gathered up what was left of her dignity and opened the door. With one last-ditch effort, she said, "Thank you for not mentioning this, Brady."

He caught her elbow. "Hey, I'll be here if you want to talk. Like I said, it will stay between us."

On a whim, Danielle blurted, "Were you in a war-torn area on the surface before you were stationed in the Holodome?"

"No, I was in one of the last cities that hadn't been hit."

"Hailsburg?"

"No, Johnstone. Why?"

With her heart in her throat she said, "No reason." They had told her she was in one of the last cities that hadn't been hit. She turned and shut the door behind her.

She hurried toward her dorm, cutting across campus. Where would Shayne have gone with her ring, if he didn't go home? She had to find him before he opened a portal. He wouldn't know what to expect. There were things she didn't tell him.

His words came back to her. *Another Maslonian knows about the Dyken takeover.* She stopped. He'd gone to see Hereth. Turning toward the south end of campus, Danielle resumed her rushed pace. He had to be there.

Students flashed by her as she sprinted down the sidewalk, trying not to run into anyone. A kid she knew from one of her classes waved at her. She politely smiled and kept going.

Once inside the building, she slowed down. The offices were on the second floor. She took the stairs two at a time. Walking down the hall, she read the nameplates on the doors. When she got to Hereth, she paused, wondering if she should knock or just walk in. She chose to knock.

A muffled voice said, "Come in."

Putting her nerves aside, she entered, feeling great disappointment when she didn't see Shayne. Hereth stared at her from his desk. "What can I do for you, young lady?"

Danielle shut the door behind her. Her hands felt sweaty. "I need to talk to you about Shayne."

His gaze traveled over her. "You must be Danielle."

She nodded. "Did he already…" She couldn't bring herself to say it.

Hereth motioned for her to sit. "Yes."

That's what she was afraid of. Her stomach clenched, and her breakfast threatened to make an appearance. "He's a fool." She plopped down on one of the padded chairs in front of the desk.

"He's just going to take a quick peek at things and come back. He doesn't believe the things you've been told. If he can take a look around, maybe see what they're doing on the surface of the planet, he might be able to get an idea of what's really going on. He's cloaked. He should be fine."

Danielle put her head in her hands. "Great plan…except Dykens can see each other when cloaked." She looked up. "How else would we be able to work together? How could we find our cloaked vehicles?"

- 169 -

A frown crossed Hereth's face, and for a moment Danielle thought she saw a slight hint of panic. "It's over, then? He's been discovered and captured?"

She clutched her hands together. "Not necessarily. The cloaking devices bend light waves around objects, so they don't appear to be there. We wear contact lenses when cloaked. The contacts show us the disturbed light waves. But they cause headaches if used too often, so we only wear them when we're on a cloaked mission and we need to see each other."

Hereth relaxed. "Okay then. There's a possibility he can succeed. If he hurries, he might not run into any Dykens who can see him."

Frustration built up inside of her. "But even if he's not discovered, he's still trapped there."

"Why?" Hereth asked, placing his hands on his desk.

"You have to get your palm scanned to open the portal into the Holodome. It won't accept him if he's not a registered Dyken."

The room filled with silence as Hereth considered this. Finally he said, "You'll have to go in and get him."

She held up her bare hand. "I can't. He has my key."

"Then you'll have to coerce another Dyken to open the portal for you."

She laughed, but it sounded forced to her own ears. "Yeah, right. The only other Dyken I know is Brady, and he's the one who reported me to Trenton."

Hereth lifted one eyebrow. "Reported you for what?"

Danielle wondered if she were limber enough to shove her foot in her mouth. "It's a long story. The point is I'm not sure I can trust Brady."

"I'm not sure we have a choice."

The words sunk in as she sat. He was right. She had to get Shayne back before he was caught. Brady was the only person she could go to. She swallowed the fear rising in her chest. She had to trust Brady; there was no other choice.

***

Shayne stared at the devastation around him. This was not done with bombs. He squatted to examine the earth. Something large had left impressions in the soil. Tire marks. The Dykens were digging here.

Shayne turned to go back into the outer ring of the Holodome, but it had disappeared. Panic arose in his chest before he realized it was cloaked. Reaching out with his mind confirmed the building was indeed still there. He held out his hands and walked in the direction he had come. His fingers came in contact with the smooth, cool surface of the stone building. Feeling the wall, he searched for the metal plate to let him back inside.

When he found it, the door opened and he could see into the corridor. It was the strangest thing to have a hallway appear in the middle of the desolate scene. He walked through and the wall materialized, shutting out the world.

***

Danielle left Hereth's office, her head in a fog. The magnitude of what she was about to do washed over her. She was going to have to tell Brady everything. There would be no going back. Her heart pounded in her chest.

When she got to Shayne's dorm, she felt desperate to get it over with. She pounded on the door for a second time that day.

Brady didn't seem too surprised when he opened the door and motioned for her to enter. "I was hoping you'd come back."

Danielle glanced down at her hands. "I need your help."

"Come, sit down. Tell me what I can do."

They walked over to the couch, and Danielle tried to breathe normally. "Shayne's powers have resurfaced."

"What?" Brady's eyes widened. "How?"

"I don't know how, but he can read minds and his telekinetic abilities have also manifested." She searched his face for any sign of what he might be thinking. She couldn't tell.

He scrubbed his hand over his face. "When did you find out?"

"On Saturday," she said.

"And I take it you didn't report it."

A tiny amount of guilt crept over her. "I didn't."

"Why? Danielle, he can't keep his powers. He'll find out about us." She sat silent, fiddling with her hands and finding the shag carpet rather interesting. Brady slowly nodded. "I see. He already knows, doesn't he?"

"Yes." She closed her eyes. She hadn't even gotten to the worst part yet.

"All right, so he knows. It's not the end of the world." He smiled, patting her knee. "They can resequence him again and wipe his memory. They know what to do to suppress his powers. I won't tell them that you knew about this for two days without reporting it." The bright look on his face faded as Brady studied her. "But that's not all, is it?"

"No." She took a deep breath in hopes it would give her both the courage and the words to continue. "Shayne took your cloaking device and stole my ring. He's trapped on the other side of the portal."

Brady's mouth fell open. "What? Why did he do that?"

"He doesn't think the Maslonians were at war. He wants to see the surface of the planet for himself."

"How did he find out about the war?"

She felt like sinking into the floor. "I told him."

"Danielle!"

"Wait. Before you say anything, listen for a second. I think he's right. It doesn't make any sense that the Maslonians were at war and close to extinction. I saw no signs of war on the surface, and I'm willing to bet you didn't either."

The corners of his mouth turned down and he appeared to be considering what she had said. "What would be the purpose of all this, if they weren't at risk of extinction?"

"I don't know, but that's what Shayne was hoping to find out. Except he didn't know he'd be trapped. Will you help me get him back?"

A small glimmer of hope grew as Brady took her hands. "Of course, I'll help."

Chapter 15

Shayne focused his mind on the thoughts of the people in the large facility. Someone had to know what they were doing on the surface of his planet. He sifted through the voices, looking for answers. After ten minutes of flitting from one inconsequential thought to another, he struck gold.

The mining is over half complete. We should be able to leave on schedule.

Shayne listened to the Dyken for a while longer, but found out nothing more. His mind reeled at what he had learned. The Dykens were mining the surface of his planet as he suspected. But why?

He continued searching the compound as he walked. He still had to figure out how to get back, but while he was here he might as well learn as much as he could.

No, not again. Please. Don't. Leave me alone!

Shayne's throat constricted. The voice belonged to a young girl, and the thoughts came from somewhere ahead. He picked up his pace.

Don't do this to me. I just want to go home.

As he neared the thoughts Shayne slowed down. The girl was on the other side of the wall. Instead of a simple metal plate, the door had a palm scanning device. This must be a restricted area. He extended his mind, searching out the room. More than twenty people lay on beds, while others walked around attending to them. He wondered what they were doing.

Hello? Is someone out there?

His heart stopped. The girl was Maslonian, and she knew he was there. *Who are you?*

My name is Maddie. They're going to stick me with another needle. Please, help. They're trying to figure out how my powers work. They want...

Her thoughts turned fuzzy, and then silenced.

Maddie? What do they want? He waited. When no answer came, he probed around with his mind, but none of the other patients were awake. Hereth would be very interested in this.

Hereth.

Shayne needed to get back to him. He started down the corridor, a slightly faster pace than before. A door dematerialized down the hall behind him, and Shayne glanced over his shoulder. A man with black hair stepped out into the hall and turned toward Shayne.

Trenton.

Shayne's blood turned cold. If Trenton caught his thoughts, he would be discovered. Shayne took off down the hall, trying not to make any noise.

***

Brady couldn't believe what Danielle had said. "You want *me* to go in and get him?"

Her wide eyes stared at him. "I think it would be best. They've issued you a pair of contacts, so you can find Shayne. Just make up some excuse as to why you need to check out more equipment. Then have Shayne follow you back through the portal."

"What if people are around when I find him? I can't start talking to myself."

The look on Danielle's face made him feel like an idiot. "He's got telepathic powers. He'll hear your thoughts."

"Oh. Right."

Danielle clutched his arm. "Please, be careful."

It was obvious she was in love with Shayne. Brady wasn't sure if there was anything to her fears about their people lying to them, but he did worry another resequencing could harm Shayne. And he wasn't there to harm people. He stood, although somewhat reluctantly. "I'll be careful."

After putting in his contacts, he returned to the living room. Everything had a slight pink glow to it. "I'll come back here with Shayne. Make yourself comfortable. I have no idea how long this will take."

She nodded, and he twisted his ring, opening a portal. Once he was through, he glanced in both directions. Of course Shayne wasn't in sight. As if it would be that easy. He walked toward the equipment center. On the way he passed several groups of soldiers, none of whom paid him much attention. Good. He didn't want anyone noticing him. But he still didn't see Shayne anywhere. He was about to get discouraged when he remembered that Shayne's powers were stronger than most.

Shayne, he thought. *If you can hear me, I've come to take you back into the Holodome. Follow the perimeter until you meet me.*

There. He wasn't sure if it had worked, but he felt better. The equipment center was just ahead, and he still hadn't seen any sign of Shayne. Hopefully he would be able to track him down.

He placed his palm on the sensor and entered the center. A woman behind a small desk looked up from her handheld computer pad and frowned at him. "How can I help you?"

"The cloaking device that I checked out isn't working. I need a replacement."

She held out her hand. "Let me have a look."

Brady dug his hands in his pockets. "Oh, crud, I left it back in the Holodome."

Her frown turned into a scowl. "I cannot issue you another one without it."

"All right. I'll come back later." This had worked perfectly. He tried not to smile. "In fact, let me fiddle with it. Maybe I can get it to work."

She went back to her computer. "Okay."

Brady left, no longer bothering to hide his pleasure. Now all he needed to do was find Shayne and go back through the portal. But as he continued to walk, an uneasy feeling crept over him. What if Shayne were walking in the same direction as he was? They could circle the Holodome without meeting.

Shayne, he thought again. *I'm almost to the group of portals where I entered. It will look suspicious if I stand there for too long. Please hurry.*

As he approached the portals, he saw Shayne rushing toward him, a dim halo of light around him from the cloaking device. *Thank goodness*, he thought. *Stand behind me and walk through the portal after I do.*

Shayne came up behind him breathing hard, but obviously trying not to be noisy. Two Dyken men came out of a room and turned toward them. Shayne flattened himself against the wall to avoid the men. Brady nodded to them before placing his palm on the scanning plate. He punched in the coordinates and the portal came to life.

On the other side of the glowing portal, he saw Danielle leap off the couch. He made sure Shayne was close before stepping through.

***

Shayne followed Brady through the portal. His lungs felt like they were on fire for a brief moment before he staggered onto the carpet of his dorm, almost pushing Brady over. "What was that?" he gasped.

"Sorry, man," Brady said. "You probably shouldn't go through the portal after running, but I couldn't stand there with you and let you catch your breath. It would have looked strange."

Shayne pulled the cloaking device out of his pocket and turned it off. The slight vibration surrounding him ceased. Danielle rushed over to him, grabbing his shoulders. "Are you okay?"

"Yes, I'm fine."

She shoved him hard, and he stumbled backward. "Good, because I am so mad at you." She folded her arms and turned her back to him.

He tried to hide a smile. "That doesn't make any sense."

"I couldn't be mad if you were hurt," she mumbled, still facing away.

Shayne came up behind her and put his arms around her. "I'm sorry for stealing your ring. That might not have been the best decision."

She tensed a little, but didn't shove him away. "You're right."

Shayne kissed the top of her head and inhaled, savoring the smell of her light perfume mixed with her shampoo. He took Danielle's ring from his pinky finger and slid it onto her ring finger.

He felt her mind soften toward him, even though she didn't turn around.

Brady cleared his throat.

"Hey, Brady, thanks for coming to get me. I guess Danielle told you everything?"

"Yes."

The thoughts coming from Brady were doubtful, and Shayne knew he needed to convince him of the truth, or they would be in danger of Brady turning them over to Trenton. "Okay. Then you know why I had to see my planet for myself."

Brady hooked his thumbs in his pockets. "I know you don't believe your race was at war."

"They weren't. Hereth's microfilm proves that."

Shayne felt Danielle cringe, and Brady raised his eyebrows. "Maybe Danielle didn't tell me everything, exactly."

"I don't have a lot of time to explain. I have to go back to meet Hereth. He's waiting for me. The short story is Hereth implanted information under his skin about the takeover, but there was no mention of a war. When I left the Holodome, the surface of the planet appeared to have been mined. I don't know what your people are digging for, or why, but it needs to be stopped. They're destroying my planet. I also found something else disturbing."

Shayne couldn't see Danielle's face, but he could see Brady, and he looked stunned. "What?"

He hugged Danielle closer to him, for fear she wouldn't take this well. "I think there are Dykens performing experiments on Maslonians."

Danielle gasped and wiggled free, rounding on him. "Are you sure? What makes you think that?" Pain showed on her face.

"I found a room where they're keeping some of my people drugged. A little girl called out to me with her thoughts. She said the Dykens want to figure out how her powers work."

"Maybe they are preparing her for resequencing," Brady said, his voice calm even though Shayne knew his mind was reeling.

"Perhaps." Shayne folded his arms. "But I don't think so. I have a bad feeling about this." Shayne paid close attention to what Brady was thinking. He was coming around.

Danielle looked like she was about to cry. "A little girl?" she asked quietly.

Shayne took her hand and squeezed it, then let it drop. "I've got to go meet Hereth. We'll talk about this some more when I get back."

"I want to go with you," she said.

"I don't know." Shayne looked to Brady, deciding to be blunt. "Do I need to leave her here to make sure you don't turn us in?"

A frown passed over Brady's face, and he held out his hand. "Look, man, I'm not here to hurt anybody. If we're being lied to, I want to find out. I'm not going to say anything until we get this all sorted out."

That was the best Shayne was going to get from Brady. "Okay." He took Danielle's hand again. "Let's go."

The sky had gathered dark clouds since this morning. As they crossed campus, it appeared to be getting darker by the second.

They made it into Hereth's building just as the sky let loose. Large drops of rain fell on them as they opened the glass doors.Shayne started up the stairs, still holding onto Danielle's hand. When they got to Hereth's office, Shayne opened the door and they came face to face with Trenton.

Chapter 16

"I've been expecting you," Trenton said as a Dyken guard closed the door. Two other guards stepped up beside them.

Shayne felt fear and panic rise in Danielle. She clenched his hand.

"Where's Hereth?" Shayne demanded, trying to sound authoritative.

Rain pelted the windows. Trenton stood, his arms folded across his chest, his feet apart. "I would think that you would have figured that out by now, Mr. Bartlet. It's a pity you're not as intelligent as you seem."

"Only a fool assumes his opponent is what he seems, Trenton," Shayne said.

"You remember me." Trenton turned to look out the window. "This is good to know. I can use that information. You are proving to be most difficult to work with. Imagine my surprise when I heard your thoughts in the Holodome today."

Lightning streaked across the sky and a large clap of thunder sounded. Trenton waltzed over to Danielle. "I wonder what you hoped to accomplish by taking Mr. Bartlet into the portal, Ms. Darmok. Surely you didn't think no one would find out?"

Danielle blinked and her face adopted a defiant expression. "It almost worked. And we found out some very interesting things."

"An unfortunate circumstance." Trenton traced Danielle's jaw line with his finger. "But not unfortunate enough that it can't be fixed."

Anger surged in him and Shayne knocked Trenton's hand down. "You stay away from her."

A small smile appeared on Trenton's face. "I wouldn't dream of harming her. In fact, I'm going to give her exactly what she wants."

A cold feeling ran down his back. "What's that?"

"To stay here…with you."

***

Brady peeked out of the window for the hundredth time. The sun set hours ago. The rain was finally letting up, the wet street shining under the street lamp. There was still no sign of Shayne or Danielle. His stomach knotted. Something must be wrong.

He stepped into the kitchen and opened the refrigerator. He couldn't eat. Nothing looked good to him. Frustration built up, and he slammed the door, the glass bottles clinking against each other.

He returned to the living room and flipped on the television. The remote felt heavy in his hand. He scanned through the channels, trying to find something to take his mind off the situation.

The front door opened, and Shayne walked in. Brady hopped up, relief pouring over him. "Shayne, where have you been? What happened with Hereth?"

"Who?" Blank eyes stared at him.

"Bald, short guy? You and Danielle were going to see him?"

Shayne scowled. "Stop kidding around. I've got a monster headache and I'm not in the mood." Shayne walked down the hall.

His relief turned into fear. They've resequenced him. Something terrible happened. Brady wiped the sweat from his forehead.

His cellphone chimed and he pulled it out of his pocket. A text message came on the screen.

Shayne has needed another resequencing. You are needed in the debriefing room. Open a portal as soon as Shayne falls asleep.

A retching sound came from the bathroom.

"You okay?" Brady called out, his heart pounding.

"I think I'm getting the flu."

The flu. Yeah, right. "Sorry, man." He grabbed his car keys from the counter. He had to talk to Danielle…now. "Hey, I've got to run. I'll be back soon."

"Okay."

Brady left, the cool night air carrying the smell of wet leaves. The steps were slick, but he didn't slow down. He hopped into his car and turned the ignition. Danielle lived on First and Ash, but he wasn't sure which dorm room. No problem. He'd knock on a door and ask for her. Someone would know which room was hers.

The first door he tried rendered no answer. The second was opened by a tall blonde with a wide smile. "Hi," she said.

"I'm looking for Danielle and Jennaya's dorm room. Do you know which one they're in?"

She pointed up. "They're in twenty-two."

"Thanks," he said.

The blonde leaned against the door jam. "You're welcome."

Brady left her there, taking the steps two at a time. When he knocked, Danielle pulled the door open wearing a large t-shirt and sweatpants. "Hi."

"Hey, what happened?"

Danielle folded her arms across her chest and shifted her weight. "I'm sorry. Do I know you?"

His stomach clenched and he couldn't breathe. They'd wiped Danielle's memory too. Why? What would be the purpose of doing that to one of their own people? He stepped a little closer. "Yes, you know me. I'm a Dyken."

"What's a Dyken?"

Brady's mouth flew open. What had they done to her? He grabbed her wrist and pulled her hand into view. No ring.

She yanked her arm away. "What are you doing?"

"I'm sorry. I think I've made a mistake." He backed away from her.

Jennaya came to the door behind Danielle. "What's going on?" She peered out at him. "Who are you?"

Brady shook his head. Jennaya didn't know him either. "Never mind. I shouldn't have come." His heart pounded so hard he felt like it could explode. "Forget it."

Danielle gave him a lingering stare before shutting the door. Brady stumbled down the stairs in a numb state of shock. He was supposed to report to the debriefing room. Were they going to tell him about Danielle's resequencing? He highly doubted they would admit to him they've been resequencing their own people.

He opened his car door and sat down to think. Danielle didn't know who she was. They've taken away her whole life as a Dyken. For what purpose? Wouldn't they have to reveal the truth to her when it came time to leave?

No. They weren't. That was it. Their plan must be to leave her here when it comes time to go.

He started his car and put it in gear. Would they tell him this? He didn't think so. He'd be too much of a security risk if he didn't go along with their plan. They were going to resequence him too. He jerked the steering wheel as he drove out of the parking lot. He couldn't let that happen.

As he drove down the street, an idea formed in his mind. It wasn't the best plan, but he had to act now.

Brady entered his dorm room and peeked around for Shayne. He'd gone to bed. Good. This might be easier if he were asleep.

First, he needed time. He logged into his computer and sent a message.

Shayne is pretty ill. He might be up for quite a while. I'll come to the debriefing room as soon as I can get away.

Next, he pulled out his duffle bag and shoved anything he could think of that might be useful in it. His hands shook as he zipped it closed. This was it. He was going rogue.

He slipped into Shayne's bedroom, a roll of duct tape in his hands. With the dim light coming from the window, he could make out Shayne's sleeping figure on the bed. He was lying on his stomach with his hands up by his head, wearing pajama pants and no shirt. Brady pushed the guilt away before pulling Shayne's hands down to his back and securing his wrists with the tape.

Shayne squirmed in the bed. "What are you doing?" he mumbled.

"I'm kidnapping you."

Shayne stopped moving. "Funny, Brady. Now let me go."

Brady pulled Shayne up into a standing position, which was easy considering he weighed twice as much as Shayne. "Sorry, dude. I can't. It's for your own good." He guided Shayne into the living room.

"Wait, are you hazing me?"

Hazing? Great idea. "Yes." He rolled up a kitchen towel and tied it over Shayne's eyes. "You're being hazed. Just go along with it."

Shayne mumbled something, but Brady couldn't make it out. He pushed Shayne outside, grabbing his duffle bag before shutting the door. The cool night air didn't bother him, but he felt bad that he hadn't snagged a shirt for Shayne. Goosebumps rose on Shayne's bare arms. Brady guided him down the stairs and into the back seat of his car without resistance.

There. That was easier than he had thought. Now, Danielle…that would be much harder. The hazing idea probably wouldn't be where her mind would go first. He entered the parking lot that he'd left a couple of hours ago. The clock said one thirty. She and Jennaya might be asleep by now. No lights were on. He'd have to take that chance. After a moment to work up the nerve for what he was about to do, he took his duct tape and left Shayne in the car. "Don't move. I'll be right back."

***

Danielle awoke to a noise in the living room. It wasn't loud, but it struck her as odd. Scraping? Was Jennaya opening the window?

The noise stopped. Danielle snuggled deeper into the covers. She'd ask Jennaya about it in the morning, hopefully after her headache was gone. She'd taken pain medicine, but it hadn't kicked in yet.

Another noise came from the living room area. It sounded like something got knocked over. What in the world was Jennaya up to? She listened for several minutes, and didn't hear any more sounds.

As she began to drift off into sleep, she felt something cover her mouth. Tape? "Don't move," a deep voice commanded and large hands grabbed her.

Fully awake now and with her heart hammering in her chest, Danielle did the opposite of what the voice said. She kicked and flailed her arms in an attempt to get away.

The man lifted her off the bed and hugged her to him, pulling her arms around to her back. "Stop. I won't hurt you."

Danielle tried to scream, but with the tape covering her mouth, not much noise came out. Her next tactic was to kick her heel up and try to get him in a sensitive area.

"Geesh, Danielle, chill out."

He knew her name. More panic filled her and she kicked violently, wrenching and squirming to get away. He held her wrists, securing them with tape, and then pushed her face first onto the bed. He caught her ankles and secured them as well.

The tape tore at her skin as she struggled against it. All of her strength couldn't tear the tape. She was going to die.

The man lifted her from the bed and carried her through the house. When he opened the front door, she saw the large screen from their window was removed and sitting out on the balcony. She didn't move as he carried her, for fear he would drop her down the stairs or onto the pavement. When he got to the parking lot, he opened a car door and placed her in the back seat.

She was shocked to see two others already in the car. Jennaya, bound and gagged like she was, and a blonde guy she'd never seen before sitting between them. The guy was wearing plaid pajama pants with no shirt on and was the only one blindfolded, although he had nothing covering his mouth. Seeing the other two in the car made her feel a little better. If they had an opportunity, together they might be able to overpower the guy.

The kidnapper slid into the driver's seat and started the car. "Sorry about all of this. I really didn't want to…um…kidnap everyone."

"Brady? What's going on?" the blindfolded guy said. His voice sounded more annoyed than anything. "You're scaring these girls."

"I'm sorry, Shayne. I didn't mean to scare them. In fact, I didn't mean to involve Jennaya at all in this. I picked the wrong room." Brady put the car into gear and pulled out of the parking lot.

Danielle recognized Brady now. He was the nut case that came to her door right before she went to bed. Jennaya leaned forward and tried to say something behind her tape. It didn't work.

"This isn't a hazing," Shayne said, "is it?"

"No. This is much more serious. Terrible things are going on. I need your help."

Shayne sighed and slumped a little in his seat. "I'll help you with whatever you need. Just let these girls go." Danielle felt a small burst of hope. Maybe Shayne would be able to talk some sense into Brady. He certainly didn't seem afraid of him.

Brady looked in the rearview mirror. "I'm very sorry, but I can't. Please, don't look so terrified, Jennaya. I'm not going to do anything to you. In fact, I'm going to take the tape off soon. Just listen to me. That's all I want."

Danielle took a deep breath through her nose. His car smelled of stale French fries.

"Brady," Shayne said. "Take this ridiculous towel off my head."

"Sure." Brady reached back and tugged at the blindfold until it came off. Shayne glanced at Jennaya and then Danielle. When their gaze met Danielle's stomach dropped. Shayne had the most amazing blue eyes she had ever seen. Even though his hair stuck up in classic bed-head fashion, he looked like a model.

"I won't let him hurt you," Shayne said, softly.

Danielle believed him. Her racing heart began to calm down, despite the circumstances.

The car sped up, and Danielle realized they were pulling onto the interstate. This must have startled Shayne, judging from the look on his face. "Where are we going?" Shayne asked.

"I don't know. Somewhere far away. Texas maybe?"

A little whimper came from Jennaya, and Shayne scowled. "Stop this right now. What you're doing could get you arrested."

Brady let out a small chuckle. "Jail is the least of my worries, bro. And it should be yours too. Your memories have all been wiped. You remember me as your roommate, Shayne, but you don't remember Danielle or Jennaya at all, do you?"

Shayne sat silent.

"The four of us went on a double date on Friday. Pizza Barn and the movie theater. None of you remember that, do you? I know you're frightened of me right now, but honestly I'm not the bad guy."

Danielle sunk in her seat. Brady was a complete crackpot. He was going to take them to Texas and heaven only knows what his plans were after that. Shayne didn't seem to be gaining any ground with him. Brady was determined to take them.

"Can you pull off at the next rest stop?" Shayne asked, his voice even. "Jennaya needs to use the bathroom."

"Wait, how do you know…" Brady did a fist pump in the air. "Yes! You still have your powers. You can read my mind. That will prove I'm right."

Silence filled the car, and Shayne squirmed.

"Shayne, man, don't play with me. You can hear our thoughts, right?"

Shayne's head sunk. "Yes."

Danielle watched her one chance at freedom flush down the toilet. Shayne was as crazy as Brady.

Shayne examined Danielle, a pained look on his face. "Please don't think I'm crazy."

A good guess, Danielle thought. *There's no way he can really read my mind.*

"I don't know how, but I can hear all of your thoughts," Shayne said.

"It's because you're Maslonian." Brady said. "Jen is Maslonian, too, but her powers have been suppressed."

"Listen, I'm not saying I believe you, but I want to know more about what's going on. I can tell you honestly believe what you're saying."

They're both crazy and I'm going to die.

"You're not going to die, Danielle. And, Brady, Jennaya really needs to use the bathroom."

Okay, if you can read my mind, say, "Bananas, apples and oranges."

"Bananas, apples and oranges?"

"What?" Brady asked.

Seriously? You can read my mind?

"Nothing. Danielle's just testing me out."

Brady snickered. "All right. There's a rest stop up here. I'll take the tape off if you promise to just hear me out. No running or screaming or anything. If they find out where we are, we're in a lot of danger. Got it?"

Danielle nodded and Shayne said, "They agree."

Chapter 17

Danielle stood barefoot at the faucet and ran cold water over her stinging wrists. At least they weren't bleeding. Still, it would take a day or two for the redness to dissipate and swelling to go down.

A toilet flushed and Jennaya came out of the stall; her pink flannel pajamas covered in bunnies made her look a bit ridiculous. "Do you think they're both nut cases?"

"Yes."

"I don't know," Jennaya said. "Shayne did read our minds."

"Yeah, neat little trick. I have no idea how he did that."

Jennaya pressed the button on the soap dispenser and stuck her hands under the automatic faucet. "Part of me thinks we should run as fast as we can away from these loonies." She shook her hands in front of the dryer. "But the other part of me wants to know what this Brady guy has to say."

"Yeah, what if our memories *have* been erased?" Danielle said sarcastically.

"It's not impossible. The government has done it before," Jennaya said, her eyes big.

"How would the government benefit from erasing a date from our memories, Jennaya? That just sounds so lame. I'd be more inclined to believe these nut cases concocted a crazy scheme to get us to go with them." After hearing it come out of her mouth, she realized how much that made sense. These guys were working together to convince them to go willingly. She had no reason at all to trust either one of them.

"What should we do?"

"Maybe there's a window we can climb out of. They'll be waiting by the door, and we can sneak around to the other side. Then we can flag down a car." This plan might actually work. It was better than sticking with the two crazies. The only issue might be their bare feet. But if they flagged down a car, they'd be rescued.

"Yes. We can climb out of a window. Good plan." Jennaya turned and stalked past the stalls to the large handicapped one on the end. Danielle followed close behind, avoiding the wet puddles on the concrete floor. When she entered, she saw a small window about six feet off the ground set into the white brick.

"We're going to have to stand on the toilet to reach it," Jennaya said.

Danielle's heart sank. "You might be able to, but I think I'm too short, even standing on the toilet."

Jennaya climbed up on the plastic seat. "Is there something you can put on top of this?"

"I'll check." Danielle whipped around and ran straight into Shayne's bare chest, his arms wrapping around her.

"Oh!"

Shayne let go and stepped back. "Sorry. I didn't mean to scare you."

Anger arose in her. Anger for being taken in the middle of the night, for getting caught trying to sneak out, and for thinking Shayne looked particularly good with his shirt off. "And what did you think forcing us into the car would do? Did you think your little plan would work? That we'd just go with you two willingly?"

"Hey, that was not my plan."

"Sure. And I'm supposed to believe that. I'll bet you boys thought you could make us trust you, if one of you were tied up too. All the while you're the only one without your mouth covered so you can be telling Brady to stop and let the girls out." Her anger got the better of her, and she shoved Shayne. Unfortunately, with the slick floor, all she managed was falling flat on her behind.

"Whoa, be careful." Shayne leaned over and extended his hand. "Are you okay?"

With her pride bruised more than her backside, she took his hand and let him pull her up. "No, I'm *not* okay. I'm tired, I have a headache, my wrists hurt, and I want to go home. I'm in my sweat pants, for Pete's sake." Her voice echoed off the concrete.

"I'm sorry," Shayne said, "but I think we should hear Brady out. I know he's not making much sense, but I can hear his thoughts. He really thinks we're in danger."

Jennaya jumped down from the toilet, her feet slapping on the concrete. "If Brady wanted us to listen to him, maybe it would have been better to just knock on our door. Breaking in and forcing us to go with him wasn't the right way to make us want to trust him."

"There was no time," Brady said, and everyone turned to look at him. "I was called in to the debriefing room. They were going to erase my memory as well. Then they could continue on with their plan."

The appearance of Brady sent a jolt of annoyance through Danielle. "Which is what exactly? Who are they and what is their plan?"

Brady's face fell. "I'm not exactly sure what their plan is."

Danielle rolled her eyes. "Oh, you really thought this through, didn't you?"

"Listen," Brady said, rubbing his hands together. "I'm not from this planet. And I can prove it." He reached into his pocket and withdrew an object. "Watch."

He fiddled with the object and his body vanished. He was there one second and gone the next.

Danielle's mouth dropped. "What the…?"

"Holy cow. That's the coolest thing ever," Jennaya said, grinning.

"This is a cloaking device," Brady's voice said from where he had been standing. "I'm a Dyken. We have technology that enabled us to capture the people on this planet. This place is not Earth. We're inside of a fake holographic world made to look like Earth." He reappeared, still holding the device in his hand. "Danielle, you're a Dyken also."

Before Danielle had time to say anything, Shayne took a step toward Brady. "Wait, go back. When you talked about capturing people, I saw something. Almost like a vision. I think it came from you."

"You can see my memories?"

"Apparently," Shayne said. "If you're thinking about them."

The bathroom door opened and two tired-looking women entered. "Oh!" one of them exclaimed, her hand going up to her mouth.

"Sorry," Shayne said. "We were just leaving."

The other woman looked down her nose at them and muttered, "Kids these days."

Danielle had a split second to figure out what she would do. She could follow Shayne and Brady back to the car and go with them, even though they might be totally crazy. Or she could implore these two women for help. She felt fairly confident she could get away from the boys now with these two ladies.

Brady's cheeks flushed pink. "I apologize, ma'am." He bowed his head and shuffled past them with Shayne right on his heels. They almost looked sheepish. And then it hit her. She wasn't afraid of them. They wouldn't hurt her.

She exited the bathroom and followed them to the car with Jennaya behind her. The cold pavement froze her feet. Shayne opened the back door and stepped aside.

"Can I have some socks and shoes?" she asked after climbing in.

Shayne slid in next to her. "I'll second that. We need to stop and get some clothes."

Jennaya got in the front, and Brady swiveled in his seat. "Yeah, we'll stop somewhere. I've got cash."

***

Shayne put his arm on the back of the seat. Before the girls decided to climb out of the window, he and Brady had been talking. Brady confessed that Shayne and Danielle were a couple previous to losing their memories. In fact, he said Danielle was in love with him. It was a strange feeling, looking at a girl he didn't recognize and knowing they had been involved. How involved? He wasn't sure.

Danielle's large green eyes peered up at him. "Do you mind if I lay down? I'm tired." The motion of the vehicle was lulling him to sleep as well.

"Sure. You can lay your head on my leg if you want."

"No, that's okay. I don't want to impose." Danielle curled up on the seat, her feet toward him. "I just need some sleep. Maybe this headache will go away." Yeah. Headache. He totally understood that. His head felt like it had been hit by a boulder.

Jennaya looked back. "I've got a headache too."

"I'm sure Shayne does also," Brady said. "It's a side effect of the resequencing."

"Resequencing?" Shayne asked.

"Oh, sorry. That's what they call it when they mess with your memories. You probably feel worse than the girls because this is your third one."

"Third? Why?" A horrible feeling settled in his gut.

Brady flipped on his turn signal to get around a truck. "The first one didn't work so well. You were starting to remember things. The second worked fine, but your powers surfaced and you found out about the Dykens. I don't think they realized your powers had returned, or they would have done something to suppress them."

Brady's words filtered in through the haze of his tired mind. "You said you and Danielle were Dykens. I'm a little confused. Who are the people changing my memories?"

Brady started in on the story of their planet, the Dyken takeover, how they were placed into the Holodome, and what he knew of their deception to their own people. After a while Brady's voice got softer and Shayne felt his consciousness fade.

"Can we talk about this more tomorrow? I think the girls are asleep, and I'm almost there myself," Shayne said.

"Sure, bro. Get some sleep. I'll keep driving. I've got adrenalin to keep me going."

The next thing Shayne knew the sun was shining in the car windows. Danielle was snuggled up beside him, sleeping with her head resting on his bare shoulder, and there were plastic shopping bags by his feet. It looked like they were still on the interstate.

"Brady?" Shayne said quietly. "Are we the only ones awake?"

"Yep. I got you guys some clothes. You were all so peaceful I didn't want to wake you and ask what size to get, so I just guessed. Hopefully it will be okay."

Shayne didn't want to move and wake Danielle, so he just peeked at the sacks. Looked like jeans and t-shirts. Sounded good to him.

Danielle's soft hair tickled his skin. He brushed it out of her face. She looked so peaceful and trusting. He wondered if he would ever get his memories with her back.

She stirred and opened her eyes. "Oh, I'm sorry," she said, scooting over to her side of the car and fussing with her hair.

"No problem. You can sleep on me anytime." Gah. That came out wrong. He felt his cheeks redden.

Danielle ignored his comment and continued to preen herself. "I must look awful."

"No, that's not the word I would use." He flashed what he hoped was a charming grin at her.

She gave him a half-smile. "Thanks."

Their conversation must have been enough to wake Jennaya because she turned around and gawked at them. "No flirting in the back seat."

"Well, that's not going to make this trip any fun," Shayne said.

Brady laughed. "They can't help it. Destiny and all that. They were boyfriend/girlfriend before their memories were erased."

"What?" Danielle stopped messing with her hair to stare up at the back of Brady's head.

Shayne cringed. He was hoping Brady wouldn't mention that. It might make Danielle feel awkward around him.

"Yeah, you two were inseparable."

No. Way. What lucky lottery did I win?

A chuckle escaped his chest and Danielle turned to him, eyes flashing. "You think it's funny that I was your girlfriend?"

He wiped the smile from his face. "No. Not at all."

Danielle frowned and stared out of the window. "Where are we anyway?"

Brady glanced back. "Nebraska. I decided to just drive until we had a plan."

"How big is this holographic place?" Danielle asked.

"Very large. Everything in the Holodome is compressed down to a microscopic level. Think of *Horton Hears a Who*. Right now we're living on that speck of dust."

"Wow," Jennaya said. "That's creepy. What are we going to do? When we're caught they'll simply erase our memories and we're back to living fake lives, not knowing about the takeover."

Brady sat silent for a few moments. "That's why we can't get caught."

Chapter 18

Nolan followed Kellec across the dusty plain, their shoes making impressions in the red soil. They avoided the craters where trees had been. Nolan pulled a cloth from his pocket and wiped his face. "Where is this Holodome?"

Kellec scanned the horizon and pointed. "Over there, where the ground is flat and appears packed down."

A huge circular depressed area sat in the middle of the desolation. It was larger than several of his city blocks. "There's a structure there?"

"Yes."

"Amazing."

Kellec squinted at him. "We'd better activate your cloaking device now. There could be people coming and going. If someone sees you cloaked, they'll assume you're a Dyken soldier, especially since you're wearing my outfit." He fiddled with one of the gadgets on Nolan's belt and a strange sensation surrounded him, as if his skin was now full of static electricity.

"Now remember, I lost my contacts, so I can't see you. Stick with me or you'll be in trouble."

"Got it."

"The plan is for me to go in, get my orders, and then you'll come into the Holodome behind me. I'm sure they'll be asking why I'm so late reporting in and why my last mission failed. Hopefully they'll believe my story about being ambushed. I have no physical proof. Your wife took care of that."

Nolan chuckled. "Want me to hit you?"

"No, thanks." Kellec flashed a grin at him.

***

Danielle slipped into the third pair of jeans Brady purchased for her, struggling to get them on while trying not to fall into the toilet. The cuffs hung down past her heel. At least the waist fit, unlike the last two pair. She hiked them up and stuffed her feet into the tennis shoes. Too big, also. What did she look like, an elephant? Oh well, they'd have to do.

She left the bathroom stall to find Jennaya at the mirror looking like a fashion model. "The clothes Brady picked for you certainly fit well," Danielle said, tugging at her frumpy t-shirt.

"Yours are…fine."

"Liar." Danielle combed through her hair with her fingers. At least it wasn't standing on end today.

"So, you and Shayne, huh?" Jennaya wiggled her eyebrows.

"Yeah, he looked real happy about that." Danielle scowled at herself in the mirror. "He's probably wondering what he was thinking."

"Come on. He was flirting with you." Jennaya tucked her short cropped hair behind her ears.

"You think?" Danielle wasn't so sure.

"Definitely. And he's hot." Jennaya gathered up their pajamas, stuffed them in a sack and grabbed Danielle's arm. "Let's go."

They pushed open the swinging door. Shayne was leaning against the rest stop wall outside the bathroom, wearing a white t-shirt and jeans. A strong sense of déjà vu reeled through her.

Shayne lifted an eyebrow. "You okay?"

"I'm fine. I just had this feeling like I've been here before with you."

Shayne pushed himself off the wall. "Really? Do you think you're remembering something?" He came over to her and put his hands on her shoulders, staring into her face.

She closed her eyes and tried to grasp what it was that gave her the feeling of déjà vu. It was almost there. She concentrated, but whatever it was dissipated. Like trying to hold on to smoke, it wisped away and evaporated. She gazed up at him. "I don't think so."

"Oh." Shayne's hands dropped to his sides.

Brady came around the corner. "Anybody hungry? There's a vending machine if you want a snack, or we can stop and eat in a few miles."

"I'm starving," Shayne said. "I feel a lot better than I did last night. What about you, ladies?"

"I could eat." Jennaya ran a hand through her hair. "Let's find a mom-and-pop diner or something. I need a cup of coffee."

***

They all piled out of the car and shuffled into the small pancake house. Shayne inhaled, savoring the smell of bacon. A plump woman with a white apron and a large smile led them to a table in the corner. The girls took one side, so the guys sat opposite them. Brady looked around. "I think we're safe to talk here."

Besides one man sipping coffee at the front of the restaurant, they were alone. "You're probably right," Shayne said.

A tall waitress appeared beside their table. "What can I get for you?" She pulled a note pad and a pencil out of her apron pocket.

As they ordered, Shayne watched Danielle. A sprinkling of freckles across her nose gave her a playful appearance. The smile on her face brightened the entire room. He could see why he had been attracted to her.

She caught his blatant stare and blushed. His fingers itched to reach across the table and touch her hand, but he didn't. Instead, he glanced up at the waitress. "Do you have something I could color on while we wait?"

The waitress blinked. "What?"

Keeping a straight face, Shayne said, "I like to color with crayons while I wait for my food." The corners of Danielle's mouth twitched.

"Well, we…uh, have a kids menu," the girl stammered, trying to figure out if he was serious or not.

Shayne frowned. "I don't like the little kid ones." He stared at her with wide eyes. "Do you have any adult coloring pictures?"

Brady coughed into his fist, and Jennaya hid behind her menu. The waitress shifted uncomfortably. "Um…"

A tiny high pitched noise came from behind Jennaya's menu, and then everyone burst out laughing.

"Funny," the waitress said. She smirked and then left.

***

Kellec tried to swallow the lump forming in his throat. The walls in the sterile white room seemed to close in on him. General Stott came around the desk and stopped several inches from Kellec's face. "Your partner came back last week, reporting your loss. We thought you had died."

"I'm sorry I didn't come in sooner, sir. I was unconscious for several days, and after that I was disoriented."

General Stott nodded, a contemplative look on his face. "You aren't in your uniform."

"No, sir. I changed at an abandoned house." Did his voice betray his lies? He cleared his throat. "I'm healed and ready to take on my next assignment, sir."

Beads of sweat formed on his forehead as General Stott squinted at him. Finally Stott turned around and picked up a file on his desk. "You came at an opportune time, Kellec. We need you to help us find a Dyken who has gone missing."

"Missing, sir?"

Stott ignored his question and opened the file. "This Dyken," he said, handing a photograph to Kellec, "has gone AWOL. He's taken several Maslonians with him. We fear he is not stable. He needs to be found immediately."

While he stared at the photo, a surge of hope ran through him. Had this guy found out what was going on? Kellec stood a little taller. "Where was he last seen, sir?"

"His last known location was in Kansas, although we suspect he left the state. You'll need some equipment. If he can be apprehended quietly, that would be the best solution."

"Yes, sir."

"All Dykens are on alert to watch out for him. As soon as he is spotted, you can use the portal and transport directly to his location." Stott handed him three other photographs. "These are the Maslonians who are also missing. They will need to be brought in and resequenced."

Kellec stared at the pictures, trying to set them to memory. These people could help him and Nolan.

"You will be working directly with Trenton."

His head snapped up and his chest tightened. "Trenton?"

"He is in the Holodome now. You will report to him immediately. I will notify him that you will arrive after obtaining your equipment."

With head swirling, Kellec nodded, trying to figure out what he was going to do now. "Yes, sir."

"I'll send the orders to the equipment center. They'll have your things ready when you get there."

Kellec left the room, disappointment tasting bitter in his mouth. *Nolan, Trenton is Maslonian. You cannot follow me into the Holodome. He will sense your thoughts. You will need to leave. Go back to Celeste. I'll try to do something from in here.*

He felt a pat on the back as he walked and knew Nolan acknowledged his request. By the time he got to the equipment center, he hoped Nolan was gone.

***

Danielle stuffed another bite of syrupy pancake into her mouth while trying to be lady-like.

It wasn't working. She was starving and the food tasted so good. Shayne didn't seem to notice her shoving forkfuls of egg and pancake into her pie hole.

Brady leaned forward on the table. "I've got an idea, if you guys want to hear it."

All eyes focused on him. "I've been thinking. Shayne can't be the only one whose powers have resurfaced."

Danielle stopped, her fork hanging in the air and syrup dripping onto her plate. "Really? You think there are others?"

Brady shrugged. "I don't know. But if there are, we need to find them."

Shayne bit off a piece of bacon and waved it in Brady's direction. "How're we gonna do that?"

"We can search the internet and the tabloids. If someone has super powers, I'm guessing those are the first places the news will hit."

The look on Jennaya's face made Danielle grin. She shoved Jennaya's arm. "What?"

"I was just wondering what my power is. I mean, every Maslonian has a different one, right?"

"All Maslonians are telepathic. The other powers vary. That's all I know about it," Brady said. "Shayne also has telekinetic abilities."

Shayne's eyebrows shot up. "I do?"

Laughter bubbled out of Danielle. "You didn't even know?"

A stark expression crossed Shayne's face. "No." He leaned closer to Brady. "How does that work?"

"How in the world would I know?"

Jennaya grabbed the saltshaker and placed it in the middle of the table. "Make this move," she said, her eyes bright.

Shayne squinted at the table. The saltshaker slid across the laminate and Danielle reached out and caught it before it fell on the floor.

"Awesome!" Jennaya said.

A smile cracked Shayne's face, and he glanced at Danielle. Her heart sped up. If she could bottle how his blue eyes made her feel, she would be a millionaire.

"Keep practicing that," Brady said. "It might come in handy."

Several people entered, making the bell on the door chime. They subconsciously leaned a little closer to each other. The waitress walked over to their table. "Is everything to your liking?"

"Delicious," Danielle said. The others nodded.

"Does anyone need anything else?"

When no one spoke, Brady said, "I think we're good."

"Okay, here's your check." She placed a small folder on the table.

After she left, Brady pushed his empty plate back and folded his arms across his chest. "I left my phone at home in case they could track us with it, so we'll need to find a library to get on the internet."

Shayne gripped the table and whipped his head around. "We've got to leave. Now."

"What? Why?" Brady asked.

The Overtaking

"There's a Dyken here. We've been recognized. He's calling it in right now." Fear leapt into Danielle's throat. They all stood and Brady threw some bills on the table. "Let's go."

***

The small, apartment style dorm room appeared to be like any other student housing that Kellec had been in. Worn furniture and bare walls, and shag carpet that probably should be replaced. Everything had a slight pink hue to it, due to the contacts. He and Trenton were both cloaked. Kellec wandered around the living room while Trenton concentrated, apparently listening in on the thoughts of the students in the building.

"Nothing. No one here knows anything." A chime sounded and Trenton pulled the phone from his pocket and stared at the screen. "They've been spotted." He stalked toward Kellec. "Open a portal. The others will meet us there."

Kellec's pulse raced. "Yes, sir." He twisted his ring and a portal opened. They stepped through into the bright hallway. The buzz of the portal stopped when Trenton pressed the red button.

Staring at his phone, Trenton transferred the coordinates to the portal's keypad and it once again buzzed alive. Kellec followed Trenton through.

Chapter 19

They had to get out, and now. Shayne took the lead, rushing out of the restaurant into the chilly morning air. He stopped mid-stride when the rectangle of light appeared directly in front of him. What the...? A second rectangle materialized several paces to the left.

"Run!" Brady shouted, sprinting in the opposite direction from the light.

Shayne turned to follow Brady, but as he did his extremities began to tingle. The feeling intensified and he could no longer use his muscles. He fell to the concrete.

A scream sounded. *Danielle.* His heart jumped into his throat. Something cold pressed against the skin on his arm and he lost consciousness.

Shayne was mildly aware of the passage of time through a cloud of haze. Someone moaned softly beside him. Pain began like a whisper but intensified until he could no longer ignore it. His eyelids fluttered open.

Light poured down on him and he squinted against the brightness of it. He lifted his hand, wiggling his fingers. At least he could move.

Sitting up, he peered around the small enclosure. Nothing but four white walls surrounded him. Brady, Jennaya and Danielle lay on the floor next to him. They all stirred.

Shayne wiggled Brady's foot until he sat up. "Where are we?" Shayne asked.

Brady put a hand to his forehead. "We're in the outer ring of the Holodome. This is a holding cell. There's a force shield over there," he said, getting to his feet and pointing. "Don't even try to break through. It won't work." He let out a sigh. "They'll be coming to take us to the resequencing room soon."

Panic flared up in Shayne and he leapt to his feet. "That's it? There's nothing we can do now?" He reached out and felt a gentle push back from the force shield.

Danielle rolled over and covered her face with her hands. "We're doomed."

"No, we're not." Jennaya jumped up. "Brady, can they hear us in here?"

"Yes." Brady motioned toward the wall beside them. "That's an observation window. They could be watching us and listening to what we say."

Jennaya's face fell for a moment, but then she brightened back up. She turned to Shayne and put her hands on his shoulders, staring into his eyes. *You can hear my thoughts, right? You still have your powers. You can use them to get us out of here.*

"How am I going to do that?" he asked, before realizing the others wouldn't know what Jennaya had said.

I don't know. Lift the key from someone's pocket. Get creative.

"What're you guys talking about over there?" Brady asked, a tone of annoyance creeping in.

Jennaya thought for a second. "Remember at breakfast? When Shayne passed the salt?"

A knowing look came onto Brady's face, and he leaned against the wall. "Got it."

Danielle pulled herself up and clasped Jennaya's hands, a smile creeping across her face. "You're a genius."

"Wait, wait," Shayne said, a sudden nervousness coming over him. "I have no idea if the salt should get passed again. There could be something wrong with the salt."

"Dude, you can pass the salt better than anyone," Brady said.

"Supposedly," Shayne said.

Danielle turned to face him, her brilliant green eyes focusing on him and causing his head to feel light. "Shayne, you can do this. We just need Brady to tell us a little more about this place we're in and how to get out."

"The force shield can only be lowered by a keypad hidden in the wall on the opposite side of the room. When someone comes in and disables the shield…well, that will be the time for the salt."

"You're forgetting a salt shaker is much different than a 250 lb. bag of salt."

Brady pulled on Shayne's elbow. "Come here." *Put your hands on me like you're going to shove me, but try to do it with your mind instead.*

That made sense. Shayne placed his hands on Brady's chest and concentrated. His mind felt the energy that surrounded Brady's form. With a mental thrust, he pushed against that energy. Brady flew through the air and thudded against the white wall, his face cringing in pain. "Ouch."

Shock rocked Shayne back. Had he done that with his mind?

"Shayne!" Jennaya cried, rushing to Brady. "What the heck was that for?"

Brady held his hands up. "Don't worry. It's fine. I told him to."

Before Shayne had a chance to say anything, a portion of the far wall vanished and four men dressed in black entered the room. Shayne whipped around and faced them. He readied himself, feeling out their forms with his mind.

The men stood against the wall with their hands behind their backs. Two other men entered, both in civilian clothes, and Brady whispered, "Trenton."

Trenton stepped forward, staring at Brady with a scowl on his face. "Mr. Grath," he said between clenched teeth. "Would you be so kind as to explain yourself?"

Brady folded his muscular arms across his chest. "You resequenced Danielle."

The smug look on Trenton's face made Shayne grit his teeth. Trenton shrugged. "She wanted to stay here on Maslonia. I only gave her what she wanted."

The skin on Brady's neck and face turned red. "She didn't want to forget Shayne. She wanted to stay because of him. You not only took him from her, you took her whole life away. You're a sick, twisted man."

Trenton's eyes narrowed. "I figured they would run into each other on campus. I couldn't leave her memories of Shayne because they were too intertwined in her other life. What I did was for her own good."

"Liar." Brady took a step toward Trenton. "You can create whatever memories you want. And that's how you like it. Total control over everyone. What you did was for spite."

With a wave of his hand, Trenton said, "No matter. This time the resequencing will go smoothly. However, your actions in the Holodome created a bit of a problem for me. There's a police investigation going on right now into the disappearance of two young ladies. It's been on the news. I don't have the time to resequence all these people. So when you're placed back in the Holodome, unfortunately, Ms. Darmok and Ms. Mella won't be able to join you."

A tightening in Shayne's throat made it hard for him to breathe. "What are you going to do to them?"

For the first time, Trenton's eyes trained on Shayne. "Oh, they'll be perfectly fine, don't worry about them." Trenton walked over to the wall and waved his hand over the surface. The control panel appeared and Shayne flexed his mental abilities. As soon as Trenton was done punching in the code, the guards came for them.

Shayne let loose, concentrating all of his force on Trenton. He flew across the room and smashed against the opposite wall, sinking to the floor, unconscious. The guard's faces mirrored each other with shock. He didn't wait for them to react. With one mental shove they all lifted five feet from the floor and hit high on the wall, sliding down into a heap of bodies.

"Let's go," he said, turning to Brady. "You can get us out of here, right?"

Brady nodded, his eyes wide. Then he noticed Jennaya and Danielle were both staring at him, echoing Brady's astonishment.

"What? You said to pass the salt!"

Brady patted him on the shoulder. "I'm glad you're on our side, bro."

The guy in civilian clothes stirred.

"We'd better leave," Jennaya said, shoving them toward the place where the wall had vanished.

"Wait," the guy moaned. "I can help."

Shane stopped and held his hand up to halt the rest of them. "What did you say?"

His eyes opened and he rubbed his head. "I know where you can go to get help, outside of the Holodome, where some Maslonians will assist you."

Danielle put her hands on her hips. "Why would you help us?"

"I found out the truth about what my people want with your planet. I don't agree with it."

Shayne probed his mind. "He speaks the truth."

"So where can we go?" Brady asked.

"I'll draw you a map," the guy said. "I can't leave. I can do more from in here."

One of the guards moved.

"There's no time for maps." Shayne took the man by the shoulders. "Think of the way."

A vision of a cave on the side of a mountain came into view. He saw the path through the forest and past the city. After a moment, Shayne stood. "I understand."

Brady pressed on the wall and the doorway opened. "Then let's get out of here."

***

Danielle followed the others into the brightly lit hallway. Jennaya put her back to the wall and took several sneaking steps forward.

"Jen. You're in plain sight. If anyone comes down the hall, there's no way squishing up against the wall is going to help."

Brady took the lead. "We'd better hurry. There could be people coming at any minute."

They half-walked half-ran down the corridor until part of the wall dematerialized and a man stepped out. He wasn't dressed in a uniform, but when his eyes met theirs he shouted, "Hey! Stop!"

On instinct, Danielle turned and started to run the other way. Brady grabbed her arm. "No," he said. "It's this way. Shayne, pass the salt. Now!"

The man in the hall flew back into the room where he had come from, and they heard the sound of glass breaking.

They barreled down the passageway, Shayne knocking people out of their way as they went, until Brady skidded to a stop. "There." He turned a corner and they followed him to a dead end.

"Now what?" Danielle asked.

"We leave the Holodome." Brady put his hand on a metal pad and the wall disappeared, revealing a sea of red dirt. He gasped.

They rushed outside, and when Danielle turned to see if the door closed behind them, there was nothing there. No time to stand in amazement, she ran behind the others, their shoes sinking into the soft, clay-like soil, a light breeze blowing dust in their faces.

Shayne was the first to slow down. "They're not coming after us."

"Why's that?" Brady asked.

"We're no longer a threat to them. They're going to lock the Holodome so we can't get back inside. Problem solved."

Brady leaned on his knees to catch his breath. He stared out across the landscape. "What did my people do to your planet? There used to be trees and grasses here."

A sick feeling came over Danielle. "There were?" She surveyed the horizon. Several miles away she could make out the outlines of trees. A silver flash caught her eye. "Hey, over there," she pointed.

The others turned, and Brady put his hand up to his forehead. "That's a skuttle. Oh, no." He rubbed his temples. "They can't be."

"They can't be what?" Jennaya asked.

Brady had a pained expression on his face. "They're taking your plant life home to our world."

Chapter 20

Nolan froze, his heart pounding in his ears. Four tiny figures crossed the empty sea of red, directly toward him. How did they know he was there? He was still cloaked. No one had seen him in the Holodome; he was sure of it. He squinted, grabbing a thin tree trunk to steady him. They didn't look like soldiers. Just in case, he could watch them from the tree line. If it turned out they were after him, he was pretty sure he could lose them in the trees.

**

Despair clung to Danielle like wet toilet paper. They were in the middle of nowhere, exiled from the only place she knew as home. Her life as she knew it was gone. She didn't even know if her family was real. They could be created memories, total strangers to her that Trenton picked for an easy way to give her a past.

She wouldn't finish school, or get a job – she'd end up starving to death on a deserted planet. As she plodded along Shayne took her hand, sending warmth up her arm.

"Hey, it'll be okay." He stared into her eyes, lines of concern between his eyebrows. "We'll find a way to get out of this."

She forced a smile, but didn't say anything.

In two steps Shayne stopped short, yanking on her arm. "Wait."

Everyone came to a halt and all eyes turned to Shayne. "Someone is here. Besides us I mean. Someone is watching us." He peered out across the soil. "Over there," he said, pointing at the trees.

"I don't see anyone," Brady said.

"I think he's cloaked."

Brady frowned. "There shouldn't be any more cloaked Dykens around."

"Hold on," Shayne said. "He thinks we're after him. Apparently he's been in the outer ring of the Holodome sneaking around. He's Maslonian."

"Great! He can help us," Brady said. "Send him a little thought message and tell him we're on his side."

Shayne grinned, and Danielle liked the crinkles at his eyes. "He can't hear our thoughts yet," Shayne said. "Otherwise he would know we're not after him."

"All right, let's get moving. We'll have a chat when we get closer." Brady waved them forward.

Danielle paid particular attention to the fact that Shayne hadn't let go of her hand as they made their way across the terrain. The group walked in silence for a while with only the noise of their soft footfalls and the wind whistling in Danielle's ears.

She had to admit that her spirits had been lifted quite a bit. Every once in a while, she would peek over at Shayne, just to enjoy the eye candy. He probably knew what she was doing because the corners of his mouth twitched a bit, and it seemed like he had a hard time hiding a smile.

As they neared the tree line, Shayne spoke. "He knows we are not a threat, and that we're in search of others who can help us."

Several moments later a black man in his mid-thirties materialized in front of them, wearing a Dyken uniform. "Hello. My name is Nolan. Please excuse the clothes." He took several steps toward them and extended his hand.

After they introduced themselves to Nolan, Brady asked, "Are you one of the Maslonians that live in the caves?"

Surprise registered on Nolan's face. "Yes, how did you know about that?"

Without pause Shayne let go of Danielle's hand, stepped forward, and put his hand on Nolan's shoulder. "We met a soldier sympathetic to us. Does he look familiar?"

Danielle watched them pass something intangible between them, and Nolan nodded. "Kellec."

"How is it that he came to be on your side?" Danielle asked.

"Come, let us go to the cave where my wife and daughter wait for my return. I'll tell you as we walk."

"Wait," Jennaya said, curling her short black hair behind her ear. "Your wife and daughter? Is that it?"

"Yes. There are others, but I haven't found where they are hiding yet."

Shayne nodded. "I hear them. There are not many. Maybe seven or eight people."

Once again the look of surprise came across Nolan. "You can hear them? From here?"

Brady slugged Shayne's shoulder. "Yep, he's our boy wonder." Embarrassment tinged Shayne's ears red, and Danielle stifled a giggle.

They spent the rest of the day traveling, discussing what they knew was going on, and trying to come up with a plan. As the day wore on, they passed through a small city, now an empty ghost town. Danielle felt strange walking through the deserted streets, knowing her people had caused this to be, even though she couldn't remember any of it. The stillness creeped her out, and once again Shayne was there to take her hand and offer reassurances.

"It's going to get dark soon," Nolan said. "I know where we can spend the night."

As they walked, the houses got progressively larger and the landscaping more elaborate until Nolan stopped at a wrought iron gate surrounding what Danielle would call a mansion. It was three stories tall with white pillars and an ornate balcony. He pressed his palm on a pad and the gate opened.

Jennaya's eyebrows rose. "This is your house?"

"Yes."

"Dude, what do you do for a living?" Brady asked.

"I'm an engineer." It seemed to Danielle that he wanted to say more than that, but he didn't.

When they were in the gate, Nolan secured it and they followed him up the driveway. There was another palm sensor at the door.

"Why are you living in the caves? With all of this security, you could have just stayed here," Jennaya said. They walked into a massive entrance hall, a spiral staircase to the right and a pair of double doors opening to a sitting room on the left.

Nolan's face clouded over. "We thought we would be secure here. We stayed safe for quite some time. We had a stockpile of food, and we were very careful. But my wife's mother disappeared one morning *from inside the house*. I have no idea how the Dykens got in. My wife and I packed, took our daughter, and left for the caves."

A look came over Brady's face and he stared at the floor. "Sorry," he said, his voice low.

Nolan put his hand on Brady's shoulder. "Kellec told me how your people lied to you. I understand now. You thought you were doing what was right."

"I should have known." The grave expression on Brady's face gave Danielle a lump in her throat. She had been a part of this too.

"We have several guest bedrooms. Feel free to make yourselves at home," Nolan said, motioning for them to go upstairs. "There are towels in the hall closet if you want to take a hot shower."

***

After a blissful night of sleep in a bed more comfortable than she'd ever experienced, Danielle found herself in a much improved mood. With the mattress and the silky pajamas she borrowed from Nolan's wife's closet, she felt like a queen. Even if they couldn't find a way back into the Holodome and the rest of the Dykens left the planet, she could live happily in a place like this. Nolan said he'd been hunting for food. She could learn to cook wild game.

And then there was Shayne. Just thinking of him made her stomach flutter. Not only was he good looking, but he was funny and–

A soft knock on her door brought her to her feet. Shayne stood in the hall. "Here're your clothes, fresh from the machine."

Danielle took the warm bundle from him. "Thanks." The silk pajamas pooled around her feet. Apparently Nolan's wife was tall. She hugged the clothes to her, a little self-conscious.

"We'll be heading out soon. Nolan said it's about a day's journey to the cave."

"Sounds good."

Shayne's smile made her wonder what he was thinking, but she didn't ask. She shut the door and began dressing. The plan was to get Nolan's wife and daughter, and head out to where the other Maslonians were hiding. Shayne figured he could find them, and the more people they had, the better off they would be.

Danielle wasn't sure what they were going to do after that. Brady had wanted to take the outer ring of the Holodome by storm while Nolan thought it might be best to wait until the Dykens left and then try to free their people. Either way, there were huge obstacles to overcome.

While she pulled on her jeans and sat down on the bed to slip her feet into her socks, her thoughts drifted back to Shayne. For whatever reason, he seemed to actually like her. Maybe it was because Brady had said they were a 'thing' before their memories were altered. It's possible he felt obligated to her. The thought made her frown.

When she entered the kitchen, Jennaya waved her over to the table. "There's dried fruit and cereal bars for breakfast."

"I also have some cans of nutritional drink in here," Nolan said, opening a cupboard. "We'd better each have one to keep our strength up."

Danielle walked over to where Nolan was standing and he handed her a drink. She pulled the tab and took a swig. Ug, it tasted like a vegetable milkshake. She forced herself to down the entire thing. Several of the others made faces, but no one complained.

Nolan packed some food and supplies and they were on their way, everyone with a pack of some sort on their back. They followed Nolan up the side of a mountain, Shayne cracking jokes and lightening the mood while Jennaya threw looks at Danielle. Half-way through the day, she felt blisters forming on her heels from her too-big shoes. She would have cared more if Shayne hadn't been taking her mind off of it. He would put his hand on her shoulder, or every once in a while he would take her hand to help her up a particularly steep part. Her skin would tingle every time he came in contact with her.

At dusk they arrived at Nolan's cave. His wife and daughter were ecstatic to see him, but casted inquisitive looks at the company he brought. "I didn't think you'd be back this soon," Celeste said, pulling him into a hug.

After introductions, Gita ran to the back of the cave. "Daddy, look what I found for Mommy!" She held up a bouquet of wildflowers, a few of the stems bent causing the flowers to stick out at odd angles. Nolan crouched down and put his daughter on his knee. "Those are lovely."

Gita stared at her father with somber eyes. "That girl has an owie."

Nolan leaned back. "Which girl?"

Gita pointed her finger at Danielle, and all eyes turned on her.

"What does she mean?" Danielle asked.

"She senses you are in pain," Nolan explained.

"Oh. It's nothing," Danielle said, feeling her cheeks burn from the attention. "Just a couple of blisters."

Nolan stood, facing her. "My wife and daughter are both healers. If you would allow it, my daughter can heal you."

"Um, I guess." Danielle sifted her weight. Shayne gave her a reassuring pat on her shoulder.

Gita set the flowers down on the dirt floor and walked over to Danielle, looking up with curiosity on her face. Taking her hand, Gita pressed her warm palm to Danielle's, and warmth flowed into her, filling her completely.

The warmth reached her heels and eased the pain, but it didn't stop there. Heat coursed up to her head making her feel dizzy but not uncomfortable. The fire inside intensified, and memories came pouring into her head, memories of her life on Dyken, how she came to this planet, her time spent with Shayne, and how she had been taken by Trenton. When the heat dissipated, Danielle was whole.

She gasped. "I can remember…everything. Gita healed my resequencing."

Chapter 21

Excitement erupted and Shayne took a step back, realizing the images he'd seen flashing through his head were Danielle's hidden memories coming back. He had seen himself in some of those images, and he wanted to better understand what they meant, but he didn't have a chance to ponder it.

"Hold on," Nolan said, putting his hand in the air in an attempt to stop everyone from talking at once. Silence fell through the cave. "This is a great discovery and one that will help us immensely. We now know how to counteract the damage done to our people."

Shayne caught Danielle's gaze and she quickly looked away. *He's going to hate me when he finds out.* Shayne didn't know what that meant.

"Do me next," Jennaya said, clasping her hands together, her eyes shinning. "Please?"

Nolan nodded. "That's fine."

Jennaya sat on the dirt floor of the cave and crossed her legs, sticking her hands out in front of her. "I'm ready."

The little girl sat opposite of Jennaya, taking her hands. Short pigtails stuck out on either side of Gita's head. Jennaya closed her eyes and appeared to be concentrating. Once again images flashed through Shayne's head, too fast for him to grasp all of them. After a few moments, a small smile crept onto Jennaya's face. "Thank you, Gita."

Jennaya jumped up, faster than Shayne had ever seen anyone move. "Gita restored my memory and my powers." She raced out of the cave in a blur of motion. Two seconds later she appeared again. "I'm a sprinter," she said, her face portraying her obvious delight.

Brady seemed impressed. "How fast can you go?"

"I can probably make it back to Nolan's place in less than two minutes."

"Sweet," Brady said, rocking back on his heels. Everyone chatted for a moment about Jennaya's power, and then one by one they all looked at Shayne.

"I think my wife should heal Shayne. I don't want to wear Gita out," Nolan said.

Gita rolled her eyes, but didn't protest. Celeste walked over to Shayne and took his hands. A current of heat radiated through him. Like a puzzle scattered on the floor, the pieces of his life began to put themselves back together. Memories of his childhood streamed past him, his father's death, his mother's disappearance, and his own kidnapping. Danielle. It had been her. He remembered how she had betrayed him to Trenton and how she left him there to be resequenced. A hollow feeling opened in his chest. How could she have done that? And she kept it from him, which was almost more appalling. What else was she lying about?

Celeste let go of his hands, taking a step back. Danielle wouldn't look at him. Everyone else stared.

"Well?" Brady asked. "Did it work?"

"Yes. I remember everything now."

Jennaya looked from Danielle to Shayne, her eyebrows raised.

"We should probably get some rest," Nolan said. "We've got to travel tomorrow."

"If Shayne can give me a direction, I should be able to find the others quickly. I can talk to them and get them to join us," Jennaya said.

The light outside the cave dwindled as the second sun set. "We should sleep now. You can go talk to them in the morning." Nolan unrolled the sleeping bags. "Maybe they'll have some ideas about how to get into the Holodome."

"Ideas?" Celeste folded her arms. "You don't even know how you're going to get in? What about what you'll do if you succeed?"

Brady grinned. "Shayne will pass the salt."

***

Danielle avoided Shayne's eyes as she walked past him to where her pack lay on the ground. This was a nightmare. Shayne remembered everything now. How she helped kidnap him, how she betrayed him to Trenton, and how she had kept the truth from him. She unzipped her bag and pulled out her canteen. The water was cool and refreshing. If she closed her eyes, she could imagine herself back on her home world before any of this took place.

She felt a hand on her shoulder, and she whipped around. Jennaya crouched beside her. "Stop beating yourself up."

Danielle stared at her friend. "Oh, I forgot. You can read minds now too. Great. Now everyone knows."

"Not Brady." Jennaya grinned.

Danielle smirked. "Nice."

"Hey, Celeste and Nolan know something is up, but they don't know any details. And Shayne…well he's dealing with his own feelings right now. And all I've been able to gather from you is that you've done some things you're not proud of. We all have. Thank goodness there's such a thing as forgiveness."

"Jen, I betrayed Shayne," she said, her voice low. "I turned him over to Trenton for resequencing. Not to mention the fact that I was the one who kidnapped him in the first place."

"Under orders, Danielle. You did these things because you were told to."

"Yes, but I lied to Shayne. I didn't want him to find out what I had done." A lump formed in her throat. "And all I can think about is his face when he found out I betrayed him in the outer ring of the Holodome."

Jennaya blinked, a sad smile forming on her face. "You need to talk to him. Give him a chance."

"Right now all I want to do is crawl into a hole in the ground and disappear."

"I understand." Jennaya fiddled with her fingers. "He loves you, you know."

The words made Danielle's pulse jump, even though she didn't think it was likely. "Maybe at one point he did. But that was a lie too."

"Just talk to him." With that, Jennaya stood and sped over to her bed before Danielle could say anything else.

Danielle waited until Shayne crawled into his sleeping bag before she stepped past him to her own spot. She tried not to think about anything as she waited for unconsciousness to come. It seemed like hours before she finally drifted off.

When she woke, both suns were up and everyone else had already rolled up their sleepers. They were talking in hushed tones over by the fire burning just outside the mouth of the cave. This would be a great time to have that mind reading power.

Her muscles complained as she stood. That night in Nolan's guest room had spoiled her. Everyone stopped talking and turned to her.

"I hope you slept well," Nolan said.

Danielle nodded, noticing that Shayne was avoiding eye contact. "I slept fine, thank you. Did Jennaya leave already?"

"Yes. She will come back with the rest of the Maslonians if they agree to help us."

Danielle bent down and rolled up her sleeping bag. Celeste and Gita came to help her gather her things while Nolan put the fire out. Danielle noticed the cave was empty; all the supplies had been packed up.

"Are you and Gita coming with us, Celeste?" Danielle asked.

"We're dropping them off at home," Nolan said. "They should be safe there now." Nolan glanced at Celeste and something unspoken transferred between them. Danielle hated being out of the loop.

After eating a cereal bar and some fruit, Danielle set out to refill her canteen from the stream. She picked her way along the path, trying not to trip on one of the many rocks embedded in the soil. She was so focused on the ground that she didn't notice Shayne standing by the stream until it was too late to sneak away.

"Oh, Shayne. Sorry. I didn't realize...I mean...I thought you were..." She stood there stammering, making a fool of herself. Again. Heat rose to her cheeks.

Shayne wouldn't look at her. He stuffed his hands in his pockets and toed the ground. "No problem. I was just leaving."

He took two steps into the woods and Danielle felt an overwhelming sense of loss. Jennaya was right. She needed to talk to him. "Wait," she called out.

He stopped, but didn't turn around. "What?"

The chill in his tone cut her deeply, but she couldn't blame him for being hurt. "I'm sorry. I really didn't mean to lie to you. I was doing what I thought was right, and by the time I figured out it wasn't right, we were involved. I didn't want to lose you by telling you what I had done."

She watched his back muscles tighten beneath his t-shirt. He didn't say anything, but he didn't walk away either, so she pressed forward. "I feel horrible for betraying you to Trenton. I shouldn't have done that."

Shayne turned to face her, his blue eyes piercing through her. "No, you feel horrible for getting caught. You had every chance to tell me about your involvement in my second resequencing and even in my kidnapping, but you kept these things from me, hoping I'd never find out. I even asked you how we met and you lied to my face."

An invisible knife stabbed into her gut. He was right. "I'm sorry."

"I know you're sorry, Danielle. You're sorry I found out. How can I trust you? What else are you hiding from me?"

"Nothing." Even to her own ears it sounded hollow. She looked down at the metal canteen in her hands. "At least, nothing I can think of."

"Great. Well, if you think of anything else you want to tell me, I'll be back at the cave." With that he spun around and stalked off into the trees.

***

Jennaya stared at the large man towering over her, his sheer bulk intimidating. Someone had called him Elisha. He stood with his arms on his hips, the other people in the cave balking behind him, probably because he was twice as big as any of them. "You won't help us?" Jennaya asked, stunned.

They all looked up at him to answer.

"We've fought them before," he said, "with heavy casualties. Most of our camp was wiped out after our last attempt. We set a trap and caught one of them, but he got away. We must have wounded him, though, because his friends came back and didn't even bother with their cloaking devices. They just rushed in and shot their weapons at us. It was a massacre. Those of us who were still alive hid in the trees. All we could do was watch as they carried away the bodies of our loved ones."

A cold fear pressed down on Jennaya's chest. "They killed them? Are you sure?"

"The weapons blew holes in my people. There was so much blood."

As he spoke, the scene played out in his mind, and Jennaya gasped. "I don't know why they did that. The others were taken alive to the Holodome."

"The what?"

Jennaya waved the question away. "The Dyken's haven't killed anyone before. They've wiped their memories and placed them in this structure they've built. We know where this structure is. Our entire race is in there. They've forgotten who they are. If you can help us get in there, we might have a chance at freeing our people. The Dyken forces are small. Most of the soldiers have left the planet. We have a chance to make this work."

Elisha folded his arms across his chest and eyed her. "What makes you think we stand a chance against these people?"

"We have Council Member Shayne Bartlet on our side."

His mouth opened a bit and he took a step back. "I've heard his telekinetic powers are strong."

Jennaya nodded. "You heard correctly. And we have some Dykens who have joined us. They've been lying to their own people. If we can spread the word, more Dykens will join us and fight against Trenton."

"Trenton Madison? What does he have to do with it?"

"I'll tell you about it on the way. Are you willing to help?" Jennaya stood on her tiptoes and peeked past Elisha to the others cowering behind him.

"I don't know. Even with Shayne's help, I'm not sure we can win against the kind of technology the Dykens have. Everyone here has a defensive power. My wife and I are phase shifters. I'm not sure how it can be used in an attack against the Dykens."

Jennaya's heart raced. "That's perfect! You can walk right through the walls of the Holodome and let us in."

A skeptical look crossed Elisha's face. "We can't stay out of phase forever. We have to breathe. We're not completely invulnerable."

"Eli," a woman said, stepping forward. She stood tall, although not as tall as Elisha, and something about her commanded respect. Maybe it was the way her hair was pulled back into a tight bun or her strict eyes. She touched Elisha on the arm in almost an intimate way. "I don't like this any more than you do, but we can't stay here forever. Winter is coming. We'll freeze to death."

"I'd rather freeze to death than give the Dykens another chance to kill us," a man's voice called out.

Murmurs of differing opinion arose, and Elisha held up his hand and turned to silence his group. "Quiet. Let's think about this before jumping in to anything."

"I want to go," the woman said.

"Asia, you'd be walking right into the hornet's nest." Elisha put his hand on her shoulder. "Think of our daughter, lying there bleeding and those men carrying her away."

"I *am* thinking of our daughter, Eli." She pressed her lips together and squared her shoulders. "I'm going whether you think it's a good idea or not."

Several others in the group spoke out against the idea. Elisha glanced around and scrubbed his face with his hand. "All right, who wants to go, besides my wife?"

A thin man stepped forward, his lanky frame barely taking up one forth of the space Elisha did. He appeared to be in his early thirties. "I will go." The rest shook their heads.

Elisha sighed. "Landon, are you sure about this?"

"Yes. I can't sit back and do nothing. I have to see if my family is still alive."

Asia took Landon's arm and hooked it into her own. "We are going. Is anyone else coming?"

No one made a sound, and Elisha frowned. "I cannot let you go alone, Asia. I will come too."

Jennaya studied the three of them, knowing they would have to do. Her heart sank a little. The more people they had, the better chance they had to make this work. They stared at her, waiting for instructions. "Okay, gather whatever you need. It is a two-day journey to the Holodome."

"Why don't we take my vehicle?" Elisha asked. "It's all terrain and seats seven."

"There's eight of us, but we can cozy up. I think that's a great idea. Where is it?"

"At the bottom of this mountain."

Jennaya nodded, feeling both excitement and apprehension. As they packed, Jennaya wondered what Landon's power was.

Landon turned to face her. "I can control the wind."

"That could be useful," she said.

Landon nodded and continued to gather his things. When they were ready to leave, Jennaya took the lead. As they journeyed back to Nolan's cave, Jennaya told them everything she knew about the outer ring of the Holodome and what they might be facing going in.

"You've been inside the Holodome where they are keeping our people?" Asia asked.

"Yes, I was kidnapped like everyone else. They changed all of our memories and made us think we were from a planet called Earth, at least how it was hundreds of years ago before it was destroyed."

"So it's true." Asia's eyes grew sad. "The Dykens are from the old country."

Jennaya felt a tingle down her spine. "What do you mean 'the old country?' You're making it sound like…"

Asia stared at the ground as she stepped over a tree root sticking up from the soil. Jennaya probed her thoughts, but they were guarded. Elisha nudged her in the side. "Well you have to tell her now after saying that."

Asia's eyes met Jennaya's. "It is what it sounds like. Our ancestors once lived on Earth."

Chapter 22

Avoiding Shayne in such close proximities proved difficult for Danielle. She ended up inside the cave leaning against the wall with her eyes closed. When they saw Jennaya approaching with three other people, Danielle sighed. They would be able to get moving. Maybe if she dragged her feet a little she could get behind everyone and no one would bother her.

"I have important information," Jennaya announced. They crowded around her, and she looked around at all of them dramatically before speaking. "The Dykens and the Maslonians are the same race."

"What?" Danielle forgot she was sulking.

"The Maslonians came here from Earth after the last great war. That is why we look so much alike. We're all humans." Jennaya clasped her hands together, delighted to share that information.

"Wait," Nolan said, holding out his hand. "If this is true, why is this the first I've heard of it? Wouldn't this be common knowledge?"

"No," Jennaya said. "Only members of the Council knew."

"I didn't," Shayne said.

Asia wiped a strand of her black hair back from her face. "You were new to the Council, Shayne. You would have been privy to this information had you been able to remain on the Council. Our ancestors felt it was important to give our children a legacy of peace, so they withheld this information. Records in the archives describe the war on Earth and the devastation it caused. So many lives were lost over pride. Our ancestors wanted us to rise above that."

Everyone started talking then, and Danielle backed away from the conglomeration. It did make sense. Why else would their people be so much alike? But, why couldn't she read minds? Before she had the chance to ask, Brady spoke up. "What gave you your powers then? Genetic mutations?"

Asia shifted her weight. "No. The properties of this planet allowed our dormant abilities to come forth."

Dormant abilities. Danielle let this information swirl around in her head. So if they were the same race and the Maslonians had dormant abilities, that meant...

Shayne cursed and everyone stopped talking to look at him. He clenched his jaw. "We've got to hurry. They're not excavating just to take our plant life. The Dykens want our powers."

***

As they hiked down the mountain toward Elisha's vehicle they discussed their plans. Breaking back into the Holodome was now going to be easy with the help of Asia and Elisha. And Nolan still had a few gadgets from Kellec. They had a cloaking device, a neural inhibitor, and an incapacitator. If they could get inside the Holodome without being noticed, they might be able to take Trenton down without a scene.

Shayne tried to focus on what they were about to do and not think about Danielle. The hollow pain in Shayne's chest worsened as he caught Danielle's gaze for a second. He knew he shouldn't feel so hurt. She had only done what she thought was right. But he couldn't get past it. So he tried to ignore her as they walked down the path.

Hearing her thoughts made him feel even worse. She continued to dwell on everything she did in the past. A few times he felt the urge to say something to her, but he dismissed it, his own pain too great.

When they arrived at Elisha's automobile, Nolan said goodbye to his wife and daughter. Everyone else stuffed their bags and back packs into the trunk and climbed inside. Only after Shayne slid in the back bench did he realize Danielle had no other place to sit than a tiny sliver of space beside him. She poked her head in the door, saw him, and blanched.

"Come on, I'll scoot over," he said, waving her inside. Jennaya sat on the other side of him, looking like she wasn't paying any attention. Right. She probably engineered this.

His heart started beating in overdrive as Danielle's leg pressed up against his, and he remembered when they sat next to each other on that love seat after his second memory wipe. Brady had totally embarrassed her, and even though he was still angry at her, a small smile crept on his face.

Danielle didn't look at him. Her expression was strained and solemn. Guilt wormed its way into his chest. She really felt horrible, and it was his fault. She had apologized and he had been too hurt to accept it.

The hollow look in her eyes doubled his guilt. He thought about putting his arm around her, but Nolan turned around in the front passenger seat and started speaking, interrupting his thoughts. He did catch a scowl on Jennaya's face.

"We're ready to go. It will be important for us to be unified as we carry out our plans. We're going to drive around to the south side of the Holodome so we can avoid the thick trees. That will also circumvent driving over the largest stretch of soft soil the Dykens have cleared out. There's not as much of that on the south side. When we get there, we'll walk the parameter until we reach the entrance. Does anyone have any questions?"

No one spoke, so Nolan nodded. "Okay."

Elisha started the vehicle and they lurched forward along the bumpy path. Jennaya poked Shayne in the side. *Talk to her. Tell her you forgive her.*

Shayne had the urge to tell her to butt out, but nipped that thought before it fully formed. *She lied to me, Jen. I don't know if I can trust her again.*

Really? That's it? Blow it one time and you never get another chance?

Shayne cringed. Jennaya did make it sound like he was being unreasonable. He took in Danielle's pained face. She looked so listless, and his guilt surged again. *All right, I'll talk to her.*

A smug smile appeared on Jennaya's face. "Good."

At the sound of Jennaya's voice, Danielle glanced up. "Good what?"

Jennaya's grin widened. "Sorry, just thinking out loud."

Danielle turned and stared out of the window. Shayne spent the rest of the trip contemplating what he was going to say to Danielle. Her deception still stung him, but Jennaya was right; Danielle didn't deserve to be dished out what he had served her. He was going to have to get over what she had done.

Talking to her now was out of the question. He didn't want to start a deep discussion with everyone in the car listening in. The vehicle hit a bump sending them all in the air. When they landed Danielle was practically sitting on his lap.

"Oh!" she exclaimed, and her cheeks turned red. She scooched over as far as she could go, but her leg still pressed tightly up against his. "Sorry."

He didn't know what to say to that, so he kept silent. Jennaya poked him in the side again and he shot her a warning glance. Jennaya jerked her head toward Danielle and her lips tightened into a thin line.

I'll talk to her later. When we're alone.

An eye-roll got thrown his way, but he ignored it.

***

Danielle couldn't believe how many times she got tossed in Shayne's direction as the car jerked and bounced. She was mortified enough having to sit practically on him, did she really have to keep bumping into him too?

Finally they entered the city and the paved road provided a much smoother ride. Danielle tried to think about the mission and what they would be doing rather than dwell on the fact that she could now feel Shayne's hot breath on her neck. Elisha had volunteered to wear the cloaking device and phase shift through the walls of the Holodome and knock out Trenton, so he wouldn't hear their thoughts and sound the alarm. After Trenton, he would raid the equipment center. Once they all had cloaking devices and incapacitators, they would all be able to enter the Holodome and take the Dyken soldiers down one at a time.

The plan seemed pretty solid. Danielle couldn't think of anything too horrible that could go wrong. Even if they were caught, Shayne had full use of his powers now. He could get them out of it…couldn't he?

The paved road turned into gravel as they got to the outskirts of town. Soon that road dwindled and they were on the bumpy grass again. They neared the clearing where the skuttles had stripped the land, and Danielle realized what had taken them two days on foot they had traveled in about an hour and a half. She could see the massive flat land where the Holodome sat cloaked.

Danielle once again landed on Shayne's lap as the car took a leap over a crater. For a second she thought she heard him chuckle, but when she stole a glance at him, his face was serious.

"Stop the car," Shayne called out.

"Why?" Elisha said, but slowed the car anyway.

"There are cloaked Dyken soldiers outside of the–"

A loud bang sounded and their windshield shattered. Elisha slumped over the steering wheel. Asia screamed and more shots filled the air. The wind outside picked up, throwing dust and dirt into a large cloud around them. More shots sounded and Brady's head whipped back to reveal a bullet hole in his forehead. Someone yelled, "Nolan, get us out of here!"

Nolan jerked the steering wheel and must have pressed on the accelerator for the vehicle lurched. Glass shattered around them and the wind came to a stop, sending the dirt crashing down upon them.

The window beside Danielle exploded and she felt a sharp pain in her shoulder. Shayne grabbed Danielle and pulled her down, sending shooting stabs of pain down her arm and through her chest. Each bump of the car was excruciating and Danielle found it hard to breathe. She squeezed her eyes shut. It hurt so bad. She could feel the sticky warmth of her blood flowing down her arm. She realized Shayne was pressing his hand against her wound to try to stop the flow.

She wasn't sure when the sound of gunshots had stopped.

"Danielle, hold on," Shayne said.

"It hurts."

"I know. Just hold on. We'll get you to Celeste."

Danielle felt dizzy. So hard to breathe. The pain worsened, and she moaned.

"I'm sorry, Danielle." Shayne must have moved closer to her because his voice was right in her ear. "I'm so sorry. I was stupid."

Danielle tried to speak but she found it was too hard. Pain. *Stop pushing so hard on my shoulder, it hurts.*

"I have to press hard, you're bleeding." She felt his breath on her ear. And then she felt something else. Moisture on her cheek. Was she crying, or was Shayne?

The dizziness took over and she felt herself slip into unconsciousness.

***

Panic filled Shayne's chest. Danielle's thoughts had stopped. No. She wasn't dead. She couldn't be. His hand shook as he pressed his finger against her neck. A pulse, faint but there. He exhaled as relief flowed through him. She was still alive.

"Hurry it up, Nolan. We're losing Danielle too."

Asia spun around, a wild look in her eyes. "Elisha...he tried to tell me." Tears spilled onto her cheeks. "I wouldn't listen."

Shayne didn't know what to say. This was his fault. He should have felt the Holodome out, before they entered the clearing. The soldiers had been wearing helmets, probably encased in trimeninite. He hadn't heard anyone's thoughts. But he could feel their energy, once he went looking for it. Had he been doing his job, none of them would be dead.

Thoughts of the Dyken soldiers invaded his mind. When Danielle had been shot he had mentally shoved them to the ground. He wasn't sure what damage he had done to them. Had he just killed five people? Conflicting feelings plagued him. Elisha, Brady and Landon were all dead. Jennaya had a bullet hole in her chest, but every once in a while she moaned, so Shayne knew she was still alive.

Danielle's bleeding was heavy. He wasn't sure she would make it to Celeste. His heart squeezed, and he knew he would do anything to save her.

The car stopped jerking as they entered town. "How long, Nolan?"

"Five minutes."

He pulled Danielle's hair away from her face with his free hand. He had been so mean to her. His heart ached to see her lying on his lap, unconscious. He should have forgiven her when she apologized. So much hurt and pain he had caused her. "Hold on, Danielle. We're almost there," he whispered.

Chapter 23

Hot fire coursed through Danielle's shoulder. So much heat, it burned. She tried to move away from the heat, but something held her down. Hands, she realized, held on to her arms. The fire intensified and she squirmed.

"Hold still," Shayne said, his voice low and gentle.

Her eyes snapped open. Shayne was hovering over her, holding her firmly in place. Celeste pressed her hands to her shoulder, a look of concentration on her face.

The pain melted as the heat subsided. Energy surged through her and the fog left her head. Celeste squeezed her shoulder, massaging the muscles. "How does that feel?"

"Fine."

Shayne relaxed his hold on her, and Danielle sat up. She was in the sitting room of Nolan's house.

Lace curtains hung over the windows, and plush carpet covered the floor. Shayne, Jennaya and Celeste crowded around her. The floral couch had a large pool of blood where her shoulder had been. "Oh," she said, touching the wet stain. "I'm sorry."

Celeste laughed. "I think she's better."

Jennaya took her hands and pulled her up from the couch, giving her a bear hug. "I'm so glad you're all right."

Danielle pulled back and took note of the bullet hole and the large bloodstain on Jennaya's shirt. "I'm glad you're okay too." Then she noticed all the blood on Shayne's clothes and on his hands. She knew he had not been shot.

Jennaya took two steps back and threw a meaningful look towards Celeste. "We should go check on Asia. She's taking Elisha's death very hard."

Danielle swallowed the lump forming in her throat. Celeste and Jennaya slipped out, leaving her with Shayne. He stepped forward, taking her hand in his, sending sparks through her.

She peered up at him. "Elisha…didn't make it?"

"No. Neither did Brady or Landon."

Her stomach clenched. "Oh, no." She couldn't believe they were gone. Tears filled her eyes and the room blurred. She blinked, the tears spilling over onto her cheeks. "Brady…he…" She found herself lost for words.

"I know." Shayne sniffed. "He was one of the good guys."

Danielle squeezed his hand, unable to think what she could say to comfort him.

"You almost didn't make it either." His closed his eyes. "I'm so sorry," he choked, pulling her close to him. His arms wrapped around her and she could feel his heart pounding against her cheek. "I don't know what I would do without you. I love you, Danielle."

The words rocked through her. He loved her? Her heart swelled and she tilted her head back to look at him. Emotion shone in his lovely blue eyes. He bent down and placed several kisses along her jaw line. His lips found hers and she could feel the passion as the kiss deepened.

When he finally broke away she buried her face in his chest. "I thought I had screwed everything up between us," she said.

"I was acting childish. Please forgive me."

"Of course." Emotion stopped her from saying anything else. She held on, breathing in the outdoorsy smell of him. It felt so good to be close to him.

Shayne took a deep breath. "We need to go talk to Nolan. We all have to come up with a new plan."

Fear edged its way into her throat and she pulled away from him. "Do we have to go back? Can't we wait until my people leave the planet?"

"I don't think we can. Since they're intent on killing us rather than placing us back into the Holodome, they're not going to leave with us still roaming free."

Danielle hated to think about her own people trying to kill her, but what Shayne said made sense. They had already killed Brady. "All right, let's go call a meeting. But first, I'm going to ask Celeste if I can borrow some clothes." She stared at Shayne's bloody jeans. "And you might want to find something else too."

He gave her a sad smile. "You got it."

***

Shayne followed Nolan into the family room at the back of the house. This room was much less formal with a large television screen on the far wall and a corner filled with Gita's toys. The rest of them filed into the room and sat on the large, leather couch that wrapped around half of the room.

Shayne took a seat, and Danielle sat beside him. He was so glad things were right between them. He placed his hand on her knee and she removed it, wrapped his arm around her shoulders and snuggled into him, tucking her legs under her. Jennaya winked at him from across the room.

Nolan rubbed his hands together, and Shayne noticed he avoided looking at Asia's red rimmed eyes. "I'm so sorry for what happened today. No one had anticipated an attack before reaching the Holodome."

Asia wiped at her eyes with a white tissue; her lips pressed together in a thin line. Nolan seemed hesitant to go on. When Nolan's eyes met

Shayne's, he gave him a slight nod, prompting him to continue.

"We need to go back while they're regrouping. The Dyken guards…Shayne's not sure if they survived his mental attack."

Asia looked up. "What do you mean?"

Shayne spoke. "They were cloaked, so I couldn't see them, but I could feel them with my mind. When they were shooting at us, I used my powers to knock them off their feet. In my haste I fear I might have used too much force. But we won't know until we go back."

"Is it wise to go back?" Asia asked.

Nolan exhaled. "Shayne seems to think we don't have a choice, and I agree. With the Dykens trying to kill us, we are in danger, even here. I highly doubt they'll just leave now without finishing us off. They know we want to go in and free our people."

Jennaya squirmed a bit and raised her hand. "I can run there. With my speed, they won't be able to shoot at me."

"You won't be able to get inside the Holodome, though. There's only one of us with that power," Nolan said.

Everyone turned to look at Asia. She twisted the tissue in her hand until it was unrecognizable. "I understand."

"You'll have to wear the cloaking device, taking over the mission your husband had." Nolan flinched a bit when he saw her face. "I'm sorry."

Asia braced herself on the seat. "I watched my daughter gunned down last week, and today I watched my husband die. I will do everything in my power to not let their sacrifices go to waste. I will go into the Holodome, take down Trenton, and collect the equipment we need."

A look of relief came over Nolan. "I don't think we should try driving up to the Holodome again. You'll have to walk."

Asia nodded.

"We'll set up camp in the cover of the underbrush on the south side of the Holodome. Once we all have cloaking devices, we'll follow Asia back to the Holodome and she can let us in."

A hush fell over everyone, and Shayne felt the weight of the task ahead of them. Their lives were in grave danger. If the soldiers inside all had the primitive earth weapons, more of them could get hurt, or worse. What they needed was a healer with them.

Nolan picked up on his thoughts. "Celeste isn't coming with us."

"She would be of great worth to us, Nolan," Shayne said.

"Someone needs to stay with Gita." Nolan's gaze shifted over to the door and everyone turned to look at Celeste standing there with her arms folded.

"You can stay with Gita, Nolan. I agree with them. I should be the one to go."

A thought popped into Shayne's mind. "Danielle can stay here with Gita."

"Why? Because I don't have a power and I'm useless?" she asked, irritated.

"I didn't mean–"

"You're far from useless," Nolan said. "You're the only Dyken we have. You know the Holodome better than anyone. And we'll need you to gain access back into the inner part."

"Exactly," Shayne tacked on.

"He's just worried about your safety," Celeste said.

Nolan turned to his wife. "And I worry about yours. You can't heal yourself."

"I know." Celeste rubbed her arms as if she were chilled. "But I am needed in this mission." She left no argument.

Nolan let out a sigh and nodded. "I will stay here, then."

Shayne stood. "We should go now before we waste any more time. The afternoon is slipping away and our light will be gone before we know it."

Everyone headed out to the vehicle while Nolan and Celeste said their goodbyes. As Celeste shut the door, Shayne saw the tears in her eyes and caught what she was thinking. She didn't expect to come back.

***

Asia swallowed the bitter taste in her mouth as Danielle clipped the small, cylinder-shaped cloaking device to her belt.

"Just press this button when you're ready," Danielle said.

Asia stared at the bullet holes and shattered windows on her husband's vehicle. She closed her eyes and nodded.

Danielle pulled out a small silver gun and handed it to Asia. "Here's the incapacitator. It's simple – point and shoot. However, you only have a few seconds after their muscles become useless to knock them out with the neural inhibitor. If you wait too long, the effects of the incapacitator will wear off."

"How far away does it work?"

"Only several feet. You'll have to get close to Trenton."

Apprehension filled Asia, but she tried to ignore it. "Got it."

"Shayne is positive no guards are outside of the Holodome right now, but if any cloaked guards come out, you'll see them now that you've got the contacts in. The flip side of that is they'll see you too."

"I understand."

"I'll be monitoring your thoughts," Shayne said. "We'll know when you've successfully taken down Trenton."

Asia nodded and turned on the cloaking device. A strange, tingling sensation filled her. She climbed over the small hill and gasped when she saw the massive domed structure sitting in the middle of the dusty plain. It was much bigger than she had imagined.

It took her twenty minutes on foot to near the structure, but no sign of any Dykens sent relief through her. Maybe they figured they had successfully run them off. Still, she kept herself ready to phase shift if she needed to.

Creeping along the perimeter of the Holodome, Asia spied the metal plate, marking the front entrance. Danielle had said Trenton's office would be about half way to the other side of the Holodome once she passed the door. She continued to walk along the outside, sending mental notes to Shayne about her progress and listening for any thoughts coming from inside the outer ring. Every once in a while she would catch a thought or two, but nothing revealing.

When she figured she was about half way around, she stopped and stared at the wall. One step and she'd be inside the Holodome. She took a deep breath to calm her nerves and let it out slowly. Then she phased and walked through the wall.

***

Danielle and Jennaya sat on a large boulder, their backs together. Celeste was standing off a short way, looking at the suns low in the sky. Danielle watched Shayne pace back and forth. It was making her fret. "Settle down," she scolded. "Asia will be fine."

Shayne pinched his bottom lip. "Something's not right."

Celeste's dark eyes flashed. "What do you mean?"

"I mean I no longer hear anybody's thoughts in the outer ring. There were Dykens in there when we first arrived. Not as many as usual, but I didn't think much of it. But as we've been sitting here, the thoughts have dwindled. And now I can hardly hear anyone."

Jennaya twisted her hands together. "Like they're just disappearing?"

"More likely they're using trimeninite to block their thoughts. But it could mean they know we're out here."

Danielle swallowed. "There could be another explanation for it."

Everyone turned to look at her. "They could be transporting outside of the Holodome."

A rustle came from the woods and two dozen Dyken soldiers rushed at them, machine guns pointed at their heads. Fear ripped through Danielle as the soldier in front motioned with his gun. "Stand up and put your hands in the air."

Celeste gasped and covered her mouth with her hand. "Kellec?"

Danielle studied the soldier. Yes. He was the one that had helped them back in the outer ring. But something was different about him. His facial expression was cold and hard. His eyes narrowed and he pointed his gun at Celeste's forehead. "How do you know my name?"

Chapter 24

The room Asia stepped into was pitch black and she had to let her eyes adjust to the darkness. The outline of a desk and chair appeared and she realized she was in a small office. If this was Trenton's office, she'd be in trouble. He wasn't here.

She turned and stepped through the side wall into another empty office, this one brightly lit. A tablet computer sat on the desk, its screen lit up as if someone had recently dropped it on the desk and left.

An eerie feeling crept over her. What was going on here? She walked through several more rooms, each empty. Surely she had been past Trenton's office by now. She wasn't going to find him here.

She walked over to the door and phased, stepping out into a long, curved hallway. Not a soul was in sight. Something was very wrong. She walked several paces before coming to a door with a hand scanning device. Shayne had mentioned a room like this. She walked through the wall and entered a large room filled with hospital beds occupied by Maslonians. Her stomach lurched and she tasted bile in her throat.

Their heads were shaved, and long tubes protruded out from under their skin around their faces and where their hair used to be. The tubes were hooked up to machines, and Asia couldn't tell if they were extracting clear liquid or administering it.

She walked along beside their beds, horrified at the sight. And then she saw him. Senior Council Member Hereth. He was stationed on the end, unconscious like the rest of them. What were they doing to them? An overwhelming feeling of disgust filled her. Shayne was right. The Dykens wanted their powers, and they were willing to do anything to get them.

She thought about trying to unhook them, but feared doing greater damage. She'd have to get Celeste in here.

A noise caught her attention. It sounded like muffled shouting. She walked to the far wall and listened. Too muffled. They must be several rooms away. Phasing, she passed through the wall and entered another empty office. From that side she could hear them more clearly.

"You can't bring Mr. Bartlet in alive. He's too powerful. What were you thinking, ordering your men to bring him in here? He could ruin everything."

Trenton. She recognized his silky voice.

A deeper voice countered, "I need him. His powers are even stronger than Hereth's."

"He'll be the end of you, General Stott," Trenton said.

"We're doing everything you asked, Trenton. My men have evacuated early. We're leaving with half the resources you promised. I've made concessions again and again for you, but I'm putting my foot down when it comes to Shayne. I need to run those tests on him."

There was a pause before Trenton spoke again. "And what about the rest of them?"

"The soldiers will kill them on sight."

"Good," Trenton's smooth voice said.

Asia took in a sharp breath. Trenton wanted them all dead, just like Shayne thought. Fury built up in her. She would not let this happen. Trenton had to be taken down. Before going in, she took a second to think. She couldn't fire the incapacitator while phased, or the weapon's fire would pass through him. She would have to enter the room and phase back, leaving herself vulnerable to Trenton. The idea wasn't appealing, but she had no choice.

She readied her weapon, held her breath and phased through the wall. General Stott stood with his back to her. She took two steps to go around him when Trenton said, "We're not alone."

Not wanting to wait any longer she solidified and fired on Trenton, taking a quick breath. Trenton crumpled to the ground. General Stott turned and pointed a machine gun, firing directly at her. She phase shifted and the bullets passed through her.

She dove out of the way, hoping to get out of the line of fire, but the General followed her movements. "She's a phase shifter," he said to Trenton, who still hadn't moved from his position on the floor.

That was it. She rushed over to Trenton, her lungs starting to burn from lack of oxygen. Stott stopped firing when she was crouched in front of Trenton, not wanting his bullets to hit him. She solidified and fired on the older man, taking him down.

Trenton grabbed her from behind in her squatting position, knocking the gun from her hand. She phase shifted as the incapacitator clamored across the cement floor, sending Trenton's arms through her. He fell forward onto the floor and swore. "I don't know what you hope to accomplish by doing this, Mrs. Walker."

She hopped to her feet as Trenton stood, a look of pure hatred on his face. He looked around, wildly. "I should have told the soldiers not to come back until every one of you was finished off."

She pulled her arm back, clenching her fist, and shot it forward, shifting just before her flesh came in contact with Trenton's face. The force of her punch sent his head back, and blood flowed from his nose. She gasped for breath, desperately needing air.

From the corner of her eye, she saw movement from the Dyken. Before she had time to react, Trenton grabbed her and pressed something cold to the back of her neck. She held her breath to phase shift again, but it didn't work. His grip on her tightened, his arm almost choking her. She struggled against him, but his strength was no match for her. General Stott came over to her, ripping her cloaking device off and disabling it.

She tried to gulp in air past Trenton's chokehold. It wasn't working very well. The General folded his arms and frowned. "I already have a phase shifter. We can dispose of this one."

"It will be my pleasure," Trenton said. He pulled her neural inhibitor from her belt and held it against the skin on her arm. Darkness came over her and she slipped into unconsciousness.

***

Shayne slowly raised his arms in compliance. There were too many soldiers with guns pointed at them, if he tried to knock them down someone might get shot. Kellec's thoughts were dark, full of hatred. He wanted to pull the trigger.

Celeste stammered, staring at the gun in Kellec's hands. "The cave…you were hurt. Don't you remember?"

"What cave? You're talking nonsense, trying to confuse me."

Danielle's face paled, and Shayne realized what had happened. "He doesn't remember, Celeste. He's been resequenced," Shayne said.

Kellec laughed without mirth. "I've been resequenced? Right. You're stalling. I want everyone over there by the car, except for you," he pointed his chin at Shayne. "You stay here."

Shayne caught what Kellec was planning on doing and his skin broke out in goose pimples. "No. Don't move," he said, maneuvering in front of Danielle and Jennaya, shielding them with his arms and torso.

Celeste took a step toward Kellec. "Don't do this, Kellec. Think about your little sisters. They look up to you," she said, her voice soft.

"What do you know about my sisters? Stop getting into my head."

Celeste raised a shaky hand to Kellec. "You told me about your sisters. Remember? You said they were still at home with your parents."

Kellec backed up, pointing the gun at Celeste's hand. "Stop. Don't come near me. I'll shoot." The other soldiers stood their ground, guns pointing at them and watching Kellec for any sign that it was time to fire.

"Kellec, you're not like this. You don't want to hurt anyone," Celeste said.

Pink crawled up Kellec's neck and onto his cheeks. "Maybe I didn't when I came here. But after seeing what you people can do…watching you kill my best friends…" His voice choked.

"That didn't happen. Those are false memories. I'll prove it to you, if you'll let me touch you."

"Not a chance, lady," Kellec said, waving the gun at her chest.

"Celeste is a healer," Shayne said. "She can restore your correct memories."

"I don't believe you."

Shayne racked his brain. How can he prove it? He blurted out the first thing that came to him. "Shoot me," he said.

"No," Danielle gasped.

He ignored her. "Shoot your gun at my chest, and Celeste will heal me." Shayne could hear Kellec's astonished thoughts. "Come on," he said, motioning to him. "Do it."

Kellec's gaze shifted from Shayne to Celeste and back again. "What are you trying to pull?"

"Nothing. I'm trying to prove she is a healer. Her power cannot harm you."

A frown fell on Kellec's face. "I can't shoot you. You're to be brought in, unharmed."

"Then punch me in the face." Shayne advanced toward Kellec. "Hit me. You know you want to."

Kellec stood undecided for a split second before jumping into action, taking his weapon and whacking Shayne in the face with the butt of his gun. Pain exploded through Shayne's jaw, and he tasted blood.

"Shayne!" Danielle yelled starting to come toward him, but Jennaya held her back.

Shayne grinned. "Thanks." He reached his hand to Celeste, and she took it. Her healing heat radiated through him, and he felt his split lip mend itself. When he let go, there was no pain left.

With wide eyes, Kellec raked his hand through his hair. "I haven't seen any of you with powers like that."

"What you think you've seen," Celeste said, "isn't real." She held her hand out to him.

The soldiers behind Kellec were obviously as stunned as he, and they watched as Kellec tentatively lowered his gun and stretched forth his hand.

The look on Kellec's face started off as disbelief, then shock, and finally understanding with a hint of disgust. "She speaks the truth," he said, turning to his men. "We've been resequenced. General Stott is lying and manipulating us to get what he wants. These people are innocent."

A murmur rose from the soldiers. Kellec raised his hand to them, a light evening breeze blowing his red hair. "We've got to restore your memories."

One of the soldiers in the back called out, "How do we know she's not using some kind of mind control on you?"

"You saw her heal Shayne," Kellec said.

The soldiers looked around, unsure, while the one in the back pushed his way forward. "That could be mind control too." He pointed his gun at Celeste's heart. "I don't trust her."

"When we were given the order to open fire on the Maslonians, Stott expected us to obey, but we refused. This is not who we are. We came here to help these people. This is not right." Kellec took the soldier's arm. "Ryan, let her show you."

After Ryan's memories were restored, the other soldiers complied. The outrage of what Stott had done to his own people spread through them.

"We have to make this right," Kellec said. "We cannot allow Stott to get away with this."

Danielle cleared her throat. "Shayne, has Asia made it into the Holodome yet?"

Shayne had been so involved with the soldiers that he had forgotten to keep an eye on Asia's thoughts. He concentrated, listening for her. "I can't hear her," he said, feeling great disappointment in himself. If something had happened to her...

Celeste grabbed Kellec's arm. "Can you get us into the Holodome?"

Kellec nodded, clenching his fists. "You bet."

Chapter 25

Shayne took Danielle's hand, a jumble of emotion coursing through him. They stood behind Kellec, who opened the door to the outer ring of the Holodome. He turned to her, the sunset casting an orange glow on her face. "Are you ready for this?"

She nodded, but he knew better. She was about to face Stott...the man she had looked up to. The man she had joined forces with and followed to this planet under false pretences. The man who had ordered her own death.

A rectangle of light appeared in front of the desolate scene, and they entered the Holodome. Shayne listened for any thoughts, extending his mind through the complex. "This way," he said, pointing to the left.

Shayne heard the soldiers behind him ready their weapons. He knew they wanted to demand an explanation from Stott. He hoped they would heed his words to keep level headed. They needed Stott, if they were going to free all of their people.

They rushed through the corridor, toward the room where the little girl was held. When they got there, Kellec placed his hand on the scanning device. The door didn't open.

"I can't get in. This is restricted."

"Let me," one of the soldiers said, pushing his way forward. He pointed his gun at the scanner and fired. The loud sound echoed through the hallway and sparks shot out of the electrical panel, but it worked. The door dematerialized.

They all poured into the room, and Shayne's mouth fell open. The Maslonians in the room were hooked up to machines, tubes coming from their heads like plastic hair. Senior Council member Hereth lay on the hospital bed on the end, his blank eyes staring at them. General Stott was fiddling with one of the machines when they entered, and he whipped around.

"What are you doing?" he yelled to his men.

Kellec pointed his gun at him. "We know what you did. How could you do that to your own people?"

Fear shone in General Stott's eyes. "What are you talking about? Why didn't you follow orders?"

"You resequenced us," one of the soldiers in the back shouted.

"I did what I had to do." At that moment his eyes locked with Shayne's, and a look crossed

Stott's face. It was a hungry look, almost a lust. Shayne heard his thoughts.

"You're not mining to replenish your world, are you?" Shayne asked.

Stott didn't say anything, so Shayne continued. "You've found the source of our powers. The minerals on our world…you're taking some of them back to your planet, but not enough to give powers to your entire race. Just enough for you. The plant life was a rouse."

Stott scowled. "You don't know what you're talking about."

"I think I do. And these people here. You're trying to figure out what makes each person have a different power. You don't want just any power. You want them all."

One of the Dyken soldiers stepped forward. "Can you imagine what he would do with that kind of power? We have to stop him." He pointed his gun at Stott.

The General pulled something out of his pocket. It looked like a trigger. "I'd like to see you try." He pressed the button and dematerialized.

"He's transported to the ship," Danielle said.

"Hurry," a raspy voice said, and they all looked over to Hereth. Celeste started toward him, but he shimmered and dematerialized, followed by each patient in the room.

"No!" Celeste cried out, her voice echoing off the walls.

Kellec ripped something from the sleeve of his uniform and threw it across the room. "Quick, take off your locators."

The soldiers scrambled to do the same, but were too late. They dematerialized and Kellec swore.

Shayne knew they didn't have time to waste. He sprinted for the door. "Trenton," he said. "We've got to get to him before he leaves." Danielle, Celeste, Kellec and Jennaya followed him.

They spilled out into the hallway and Shayne listened for Trenton's thoughts. "Straight ahead," he said. Empty white rooms flashed by him as he ran. Stott had cleared the entire outer ring. They'd be taking Trenton and leaving any moment.

He slowed his pace. Trenton was close. Shayne stuck his head into several rooms before he saw him. Trenton stood behind a desk, bent over a keyboard, frantically typing. He stopped when Shayne entered.

Danielle and the rest filed into the room, and Shayne held his arms out, motioning them to stay behind him. Trenton raised his hand, and Shayne readied himself for a fight. Something sprang up from the desk into Trenton's hand.

"That's it, then? You're leaving?" Shayne said. "What about your people, trapped in the Holodome? Don't you care about your own flesh and blood?"

"The people are fine. They're happy. They're living their lives. Leave them alone."

Shayne stared into Trenton's deep-set eyes. "Why are you doing this?"

The air in the room turned stale. Trenton clicked his tongue to his teeth. "And here I thought you had it all figured out. It's a shame you can't use that powerful brain of yours for thinking."

Heat crept up Shayne's neck, but he remained calm. "Really? You're going to resort to throwing insults?" He felt Danielle's hand on his shoulder, warning him.

"I don't have time for this. I have to go convince someone you're not as valuable as he thinks you are." With that, Trenton pressed his button and dematerialized.

"Let him go," Kellec said with a wave. "We don't need him. I can get us into the Holodome."

A bad feeling crept over Shayne. "Are you sure? Why would Trenton leave us when we can just go into the Holodome and rescue our people?"

Kellec's face turned white and he left the room. Everyone followed him to a portal on the inner wall. Kellec placed his palm on the scanner, and a green light moved over his hand. The display lit up.

Dyken 2714 unauthorized. Access denied.

Kellec swore and pounded his fist on the solid portal door. "You're right. Trenton locked us out."

They stood staring at each other for a moment while the realization sunk in. They wouldn't be able to get to their people. Maslonia was desolate…no one left but a handful of them.

Locked out of the Holodome, they were on their own.

What would they do for food? He supposed they would raid the stores until supplies ran out or spoiled. Then they could hunt.

Jennaya's voice cut into his thoughts. "Where's Asia? Wouldn't she be able to walk through the wall into the Holodome?"

"No," Danielle said. "It doesn't work that way. If you don't go through an active portal and get decompressed, you'd die."

The mention of Asia sent renewed guilt through Shayne. "I don't hear Asia's thoughts. We'd better split up and find her."

Danielle took his hand. "We'll take the left, circling back. You guys can take the right."

Kellec nodded, starting down the hall, Jennaya and Celeste following after him. Shayne squeezed Danielle's hand. He wanted to ask if she was prepared for what they might find, but couldn't bring himself to do it.

Since he had already checked in some of the rooms, the search went quickly. With each empty room, his apprehension increased. What had they done to Asia?

As they neared the half-way point around the Holodome, they heard Jennaya's shriek come from up ahead. "She's here!"

They sprinted around the curve of the Holodome until they came to Kellec standing by an open doorway, his face grave. Danielle pushed past him and Shayne followed.

He found himself crammed in some kind of supply closet, shelves full of boxes and bottles lining the walls. Jennaya was on the floor kneeling over Asia's body, Celeste beside her, holding Asia's hand. A large pool of blood soaked the cement beneath her.

"Is she…?" He asked, not being able to finish the question.

"She's alive," Celeste said, "but just barely."

Relief flooded through him. "You can heal her then, right?"

"I don't know." Celeste entwined her fingers with Asia's, her dark hands a huge contrast against Asia's deathly pale skin. Celeste's eyebrows furrowed. The seconds ticked by. No one moved. And then Asia's chest rose and she took in a deep breath, coughed, and then turned her head, spitting out a mouthful of blood.

"You did it," Jennaya said, pulling Celeste into a hug.

Asia sat up and peered down at her blood soaked clothes. "Trenton!"

"He's gone," Shayne said. "He and Stott took off. In fact, all of the Dykens have left."

"He left me here to die."

"I know." Shayne shifted his weight, unsure of what else to say.

Danielle placed her hand on Asia's shoulder. "It's okay. You're safe now."

Those words hung in the air for a minute before Celeste stood. "We'd better get back to Nolan. He must be frantic."

They stepped out of the Holodome, the cool night air cutting through Shayne's clothes. His eyes had to adjust to the darkness.

"I'll go get the vehicle." Jennaya took off across the soft soil and the rest of them began walking. Soon they saw headlights coming toward them.

In the distance, low in the sky, a ring of lights appeared. They shot across the sky, approaching them at high speed. Danielle gasped. "A spaceship. They're coming after us."

Beams of light came down from the spaceship, hitting the ground close to them, showering them with clods of dirt. The noise was deafening and the ground shook. The lights whizzed by, slowed, and then came around for a second attempt.

Shayne clasped his hands to the sides of his head, gathering up all the energy he could muster. As the spaceship neared, he forced the energy toward it, pushing it as hard as he could.

The lights in the sky jerked away and the sound of twisting metal pierced his ears. For a moment Shayne thought the aircraft would go down, but it hovered for a few moments before taking off, disappearing over the dark horizon. Weak from the exertion, he grabbed onto Danielle's arm.

Headlights bounced across the land and Jennaya pulled up beside them. "Are you guys okay?"

Shayne glanced around at the others. "We're fine. I don't think they're coming back."

The Overtaking

"I think you're right," Danielle said. For some reason that made everyone laugh.

***

Danielle rolled over on the soft mattress, tucked her shoulder under the covers and listened to Jennaya's steady breathing while staring at the back of her head. With the extra people staying at Nolan's house, they had doubled up. Danielle didn't mind. After the death and destruction of yesterday, she was just glad Jennaya was alive.

This brought thoughts of Brady and the others they had lost yesterday. Her heart squeezed in her chest and she wiped the tears from her eyes. Brady had been executed by his own people. Her people. No, that wasn't true. He was executed by Stott.

She slipped out of bed and peered out of the window at the large tree in Nolan's yard. The tips of the leaves were turning yellow. Fall. Her mother loved this time of year. More tears slipped down her cheeks. She would never see her mother or father again. Stott left her here.

A soft knock on the door sounded. She shuffled over to the door and wiped the tears away before opening it. Shayne.

"I heard you get up," he said, his voice low. "Thought you might want to go for a walk or something."

He'd heard her thoughts, no doubt. His concern for her was touching. She nodded. "I'd like that."

"I'll wait for you in the kitchen."

Danielle tossed some clothes on and ran a brush through her tangled hair. By the time she was done, she didn't look half bad. Her eyes were still a little puffy, but she didn't care.

Shayne stood as she entered the kitchen. "Come here, there's something I want to show you." He held his hand out to her.

He led her through the back door and down a stone path to a garden. The landscaping was beautiful, small pools of water sprinkled in amongst rock, trees and flowers. The path took them to a circular clearing. An old fashioned wooden bench overlooked the grounds. Some of the flowers and vegetation had died in preparation for the cold winter with no groundskeeper to clear them out, but it was still breathtaking.

"Have a seat," Shayne said, motioning to the bench.

"Thank you." The bench was surprisingly warm even with the chilly morning air. "Have you been sitting out here?"

"I needed to think." He put his arm around her, and she felt that familiar spark of energy rush through her.

Danielle snuggled into him. "What you said yesterday…after Celeste healed me…"

"That I love you?"

"Yeah, that."

He paused before saying, "What about it?"

"Nothing. I just wanted to hear you say it again."

A chuckle caused his chest to bounce, and he kissed the top of her head. "I love you, Danielle."

She breathed in the clean smell of him and allowed the words to grow in her heart. Shayne loved her. That's what should matter most, right? Then why did she still feel this hollow emptiness in her chest?

"I'm sorry you're in pain," he said quietly.

She took in a deep breath and let it out slowly. "I guess I didn't think I would be saying goodbye to my parents for the last time when I left."

Shayne rubbed her arm. "I know how you feel," he said, his voice cracking.

Guilt rushed through her. "I'm being so insensitive. You lost your mother and Brady, and here I am whining about not being able to see my parents again."

"It's okay. We're both hurting."

"Do you think my parents will come looking for me?" As soon as the words were out, she knew the truth. "No, probably not. Stott will tell them I died...that your people killed me."

Silence once again took over, with the occasional sound of a bird fluttering in the trees. Danielle could feel Shayne's heartbeat against her cheek. Thoughts of how her life was going to be now filled her mind. She wondered if they'd ever be able to break into the Holodome to free the

Maslonian people. She was about to ask Shayne when he spoke. "I think we'll figure out a way."

"Good, because I want you to be happy."

"And why is that?"

"Because I love you," she said.

He chuckled again. "It is nice to hear those words, isn't it?" He lifted her chin up and gazed into her eyes.

She might have answered him if her lips weren't so busy.

The End of Book One

Look for the *New York Times* Bestseller
Not What She Seems by Victorine E. Lieske

Steven Ashton, a billionaire from New York, and
Emily Grant, on the run from the law...and when
they meet he can't help falling for her. What he
doesn't know is that interfering in her life will put
his own life in danger. Not What She Seems holds
you in suspense from the moment you begin down
the path of murder and romance.

When billionaire Steven Ashton couldn't stand his
high society social life anymore, he left the stress of
New York on a vacation for his soul. The need to
meet real down to earth people lead him to a small
Nebraska town he remembered visiting as a child.
He didn't want to lie about who he was, but he
couldn't exactly tell them the truth.

Emily could have easily fallen in love with Steven,
under different circumstances, but her past was
catching up with her and she needed a new life. If
the authorities found out about her, she could lose
the one thing that meant everything, her four year
old son.

Not What She Seems is 326 pages and is a "sweet"
romantic suspense, appropriate for all ages.

Follow Victorine

Website:
http://victorinelieske.com

Email:
vicki@victorinelieske.com

Facebook Fan Page:
http://facebook.com/victorinelieske

Blog:
http://victorinewrites.blogspot.com